A Family Thing

Randy Beal

This book is dedicated to
my beautiful and amazing wife, Emily.
I love you more every day!

CONTENTS

Acknowledgments

Aunt Sandy, thank you so much for your support in my dream and allowing me to dream even bigger. Bob, thanks for being a great writing partner & even better friend. Michael, you keep knocking it out of the park thanks for everything. To the others that have shared their knowledge with me on this book, thank you.

617

A Family Thing

Reunion

The house rose up to meet us on the right. "Can't miss that," I thought. It was the only house on this stretch of County Road 10. I was told it would be a white farmhouse, but years of aging and weather damage had yellowed it, like a smoker's smile. One of the shutters on the second level was missing a hinge and leaned inward, as if the house were winking at me.

As we turned down the gravel drive, I realized I was excited to be here--my first family reunion since I was a child. Dad and I made the trek down from the suburbs of Chicago early that morning. I smiled to see the porch swing in the same spot and remembered sitting there in Grandpa's lap, trying to stay awake to hear his stories as the sun was setting.

Dad popped the car into park and fished in the back seat to grab our obligatory out-of-towner's bucket of chicken. I grabbed some lawn chairs from the trunk. We made our way around to the back.

I saw a lot of familiar faces that were somehow hard to place. Groups of grey-haired ladies were bunched up under a patio umbrella sipping iced teas. Some of them waved. One lady carrying a casserole came over to hug my dad and motioned a man in a plaid vest over. "You remember little Donnie, don't you?" she nudged him. "And this must be Jacob." She transferred the casserole to her partner and pulled me in for a hug.

"Good to see you," I offered generically. Dad must have realized I was struggling, so he interjected, "Jake, this is Ellie."

"How have you been?" I followed up, just as generically. Thankfully, just at that moment, one of the kitchen ladies called her back for a consultation. Her casserole-toting partner (I assumed a husband, but didn't know) left with her.

Dad walked up to a man and woman that looked to be about his age. I followed. "There he is!" the man shouted, making a gun with his fingers and shooting it. He took a shot at me, too, then blew the imaginary smoke off the barrel. Dad didn't wait for me to make small talk this time.

"Jake, this is Gail and Clayton. They live in Kentucky and they took care of you after you had that accident."

By then, the masses of relatives had formed a circle around us. Dad began to introduce them in quick-fire fashion.

"This is Jack. And yes, his wife, Jill. No kidding. This is Lewis, whom you know. He lives about two miles up the road. This is Phillip. You met Ellie and Hank. And who can forget Chester, the saint of the family?"

I shook all the hands and nodded and repeated their names and then someone put a plate of food and a drink in my hands. So I found a seat and fell to it. I couldn't wait to dig in. There was brisket, a couple of different casseroles, baked beans, and pecan pie. This was going to be a good day.

Good Times

I rubbed my eyes, the glow of the computer finally getting to me. How long had I been sitting here trying to finish the article? "Susan will kill me," I muttered out loud, though no one was in the room with me. Rachel was no doubt already in bed; she got so tired so early these days.

It suddenly occurred to me that my unfinished piece on a local charity just needed something from an old article. I knew there was a print out of that somewhere. I started shuffling through the various piles on my desk and inadvertently knocked one of them over, which fell behind the desk into spider territory. I was down on my hands and knees trying to tease it out when Rachel smacked me soundly on the rump.

"Careful where you point that thing, babe," she joked.

"What are you still doing up?" I asked without rising. "And I didn't say stop."

She smacked me even harder. "Look at this when you're done mooning me."

I shook my fanny a few more times, and rose to see what she had. A handful of swatches. Looked like she was still undecided on colors for the nursery.

"What do you think of this combo? And what are YOU still doing locked away in here? I thought your article was due at nine."

"You know I always use up my one hour grace period." I flipped through the swatches. "Seriously? You think I have an opinion between taupe and mauve?" I winked, just in case I needed to prevent a mysterious offense. "This one," I pointed.

Rachel tore the swatch I had pointed to in half and threw it in the trash. "Excellent work. Helpful as always."

I pretended to be more shocked than I was. "Why'd you ask me in the first place if you were just going to pick what you wanted?"

"I wanted to make you feel like you were a part of this, even though we both really know who's in charge."

I rolled my eyes.

"I saw that," she said. "The nursery color is no big deal, but you'd better up your game, mister, when this baby is born." She jabbed a finger into my chest.

A flash of anger rose up in me and for an instant I envisioned myself bending that finger backwards until she cried out in pain. Instead I said, "What are you talking about? I'll get the nursery done in time."

"Will you?" she paused for a moment as if deciding to push it further, then turned without waiting for an answer.

I huffed and went back to searching for the article. I found it a short time later, worked it in to the right place, ran spell check, and submitted it to Susan, all well within my one hour grace period. I should have been pleased with myself, but instead I was still in full-on stew mode with a low and slow setting and couldn't shake what Rachel had said about upping my game. Why did that bother me so much?

I put my head down on the desk to rest for a moment.

I guess Rachel's finger-pointing bothered me more than I wanted to admit. Maybe because she was right. I *was* dragging my feet: on the nursery, on being ready, on this whole dad thing, even though it was my idea to begin with. I had promised to read *What to Expect When You're Expecting* faithfully along with Rachel, but hadn't gotten past the first chapter. I did want to—DO want to--have a kid. It was Rachel who initially resisted the idea. I now found it difficult to remember the arguments I had used on her. Whatever it was, it did the trick and in her usual Rachel way, once she had resigned herself to the idea, she went after it hard core and by-the-book. She insisted we read the standard parenting books, dove into planning the nursery, reminded me at every turn how things would change. At first, it was endearing, seeing her finally excited about my dream. But her zeal got me thinking that I should be more excited and why wasn't I?

True, this was all new territory for us, but I usually was up for change, for an adventure. Like when Dad would poke his head into my room growing up and say, "What ya doing, boy? Wanna go for a drive?" He never told me where we were going. It was always a surprise. Sometimes there was ice cream at the end of it. Or sometimes we were visiting a relative. Or offering free mechanic services for a shut in. But it didn't matter to me back then. I just loved going for the joy of the journey.

I can picture Dad now, one hand draped across the wheel casually, a setting sun tinting his hair gold. He's absently tapping the lid of his nearly empty Styrofoam coffee cup while telling me a story about the work day. Traffic is swirling around us at 75 miles per hour despite the posted 65 signs, but we seem to be frozen in time as cars whiz by.

"Oh shit!" I see it a split second before Dad does.

The semi in front of us stops suddenly and the "how's my driving?" ad on the hinged back door rushes up to eye level. I hear a horrific crunching sound and watch helplessly in horror as the tailgate of the semi smashes through the windshield. Glass flies everywhere.

Adrenaline takes over and I'm out of the car the next instant. I realize my Dad has also made it out. He gives me a look as if to say, "Holy crap! Did that just happen?" But we don't say anything out loud. Our pick-up is totaled. There is no conceivable way anyone could have made it out of that alive, yet here we both are, standing beside the wreck with not a scratch on us.

I woke up instantly, relieved this was only a dream, but stunned at how vivid it was. It was the kind of dream that leaves an emotion behind even as the image fades.

I found myself missing the times when Dad and I worked together. We sometimes could go for most of the day in the shop and not talk to each other. I would be working the front desk, talking with customers, scheduling the mechanics shifts while Dad would be back in the shop with the guys, getting his hands dirty, busting his hump to make sure we got a customer's car ready by the end of the day. We might pass each other briefly in the hall and he'd nod his head and say, "Son." Other days when the orders were slow, we'd hang out in the office playing stupid office games and drinking coffee.

Ah the smell of the shop . . . smell memories suddenly permeated the air. Slightly burnt coffee was always at the base mixed in with used oil and the chalky dustiness of Oil-Dri. Food smells from the guys' ever-present brown-bag lunches wafted in and out, in particular Dad's fried bologna and raw onion sandwiches. It was rare for the mechanics to bring fast food in. They saved money by bringing in peanut butter and jelly sandwiches and a bag of chips. Dad always had a box of donuts in the kitchen, and by the afternoon one or two of the stale ones that had sat out added their doughy sweetness to the aroma party. We always hazed the new guys by telling them it was their responsibility to bring in donuts in the morning-- the good ones from Dunkin with chocolate icing and sprinkles. Before long they would figure out they were being duped and we reverted back to the plain gas-station bargain donuts that Dad could justify bringing in.

And Old Spice. Charlie always seemed to steep himself in it. He was old school that way and it might have been off-putting if Charlie weren't so darn funny. If there were outbursts of laughter floating above the clank of the tools in the shop, you could be sure Charlie was behind it. Charlie was as old as the shop itself--the first employee Dad had officially hired. He had worked as a mechanic in the Army and was always ready with a story about his time spent in the service.

Charlie was a talker, but one who could take apart a carburetor or flush out a radiator while regaling me with a story and he'd never skip a beat with either. He was no slacker, just very energetic and jovial.

"See you later," we'd say at the end of a shift.

"Not if I see you first," was Charlie's constant reply. Even though we knew it was coming and had heard it a thousand times, it still seemed funny coming from him.

It was always fun to be around Charlie. One got the sense that instead of damaging him, his years in the Army had shaped him and given him purpose and made him happy. While I couldn't fully relate to his war stories, I shared a corny sense of humor with him. Some of the jokes I still tell to this day came from Charlie. His personal favorite:

"Man goes to the doctor and says, 'Doctor, you gotta help me. Every time I drink a cup of coffee, I get a stabbing pain in my eye. What should I do?' The doctor says, 'Take the spoon out first.'"

On slow days, we'd sit around the shop and pitch lug nuts into Styrofoam cups while Charlie gave us his best imitation of his barrack's sergeant or walked us through a battle. Dad sponsored a snack tray that sat out in the afternoons: chips, cookies, jerky, sodas, and the like, provided by an outside vendor. Payment worked on the "honor system." Little did Dad know his son was eating up the profits by sneaking snacks. I always felt guilty later and would secretly pay back the balance in cash when the vendor noted how much they were short.

Of course, Mitch put an end to all that. Dad brought Mitch on initially as a temporary mechanic to help with overflow, but soon Mitch proved to be indispensible and Dad offered him a full time position. I always felt that Mitch kissed up to Dad and only put his best foot forward when Dad was there to see it. In moments of real honesty, though, I knew it was because Mitch was damn good at his job. Mitch was twice as fast and three times as knowledgeable as anyone else on staff, except maybe Charlie and Dad himself. Mitch and I didn't see eye to eye on anything. Dad moved me to an office role shortly after Mitch went full time, which meant I spent less time hob-nobbing with the guys. It was the beginning of my dissatisfaction with working at the shop and made me long for the good ol' days.

Shop Talk

The morning commute was only 15 minutes for me--plenty of time to get a cup of coffee and listen to the radio in preparation for the day. Most days, I would listen to ESPN radio, but if I was in a music mood I'd go with *The Mix*. I liked to think of the DJs as my radio family.

I usually parked next to my dad and would peek into his car to see how messy it was. It was a type of twisted mental competition I had with him—in my mind only--to see who was more disorganized. I prided myself in usually winning the contest. My dad was smart enough to schedule me to come in around 9 or even 10 o'clock most days, partly because he knew I liked to sleep in, but more because he recognized that a bit of separation between our work and home life might do me some good.

I was still living at home and not ashamed of it, but was also trying to assert my independence wherever I could. Some mornings I'd come straight to the shop from a friend's house where I had crashed on the couch after a night of drinking. My parents gave me plenty of independence and seldom played the "if you're going to live under my roof" card.

At the shop, there was a small kitchen and dining area, and some storage lockers and a changing room behind that. I didn't have my own official embroidered mechanic shirt like my dad and Charlie did, but I did fit into some of my dad's old shirts and sometimes wore them. The guys would call me Don and mock salute me on those days, and I would pretend to boss them around.

After changing, I would punch in and check in to see what Dad needed. At first, it was pretty much janitorial stuff, but after a few months, I went straight to the shop and shadowed either Dad or Charlie. I preferred the days I got to work with Charlie, mainly because I didn't want to be perceived as the boss's kid and get special treatment, even though that's pretty much what I got.

Charlie would take an appraising look at me on those mornings and shake his head slowly back and forth and say something like "I can see I've really got my work cut out for me today. Well, get over here, soldier!"

His drill sergeant routine might include phrases like, "I said 5/8ths, Maggot!" or "Drop and give me the components of a carburetor!" and I would have to shout out the parts with a hearty "Sir, Yes, Sir!" at the end.

13

Charlie had no qualms with dirt and even less with getting me dirty. There were days when I would stand at the changing room sink and try to wash the grease off my hands for ten minutes straight and still leave feeling greasy and gross. I could live with a messy car or let the laundry pile up in my bedroom, but when the dirt got on me or my clothes, I had a tougher time dealing with it. Charlie would grill me for my "clean as I go" approach, but I couldn't help it.

In the afternoons, my brother John would stop by after school to help with odd jobs around the shop. I tried to wear my dirty uniform as a badge of honor around him, secretly gratified that he was now playing the role of errand boy that I used to play — the lowest man on the totem pole. But I was a mechanic, even if I still had my training wheels on. I enjoyed seeing John doing these menial tasks, and you would think that was good enough for me, but I found myself still playing the big brother role, giving him grief, and making his job tougher. After he swept an area, I would dirty it up. Now that's just brotherly love.

By the time John finished up his chores, we were all ready to go home, Belcher caravan style. Since we had all arrived at different times and in different cars, our competitive natures kicked in and we would race to see who would make it home first. I would sometimes branch off from the traditional route, hoping to find a new short cut or to get lucky with traffic on side streets. Sometimes it paid off; other times I would get lost and catch all kinds of grief for arriving late for supper.

When Dad had first noticed the shop, it was a failed mechanic business unimaginatively called "Pete's" that had boarded up windows and a "for sale" sign. Dad had been wanting to launch his own business and Pete's seemed like the perfect size and location. Poor Pete, as our family called him, was a cranky old man too set in his ways to upgrade his tools and methods, and he hemorrhaged customers as a result. As less and less business trickled in, Pete shut down one wing of the building, which basically became a used part grave yard.

Poor Pete was only too glad to offload his shop, and Dad got it for a steal. For months, Dad and Charlie (whom Dad had already promised a head mechanic spot) focused on the getting the operational half of the building, well, operational. It was in decent enough shape to get their business started, but Dad always had designs on the closed off wing. He knew if he could just clear those additional bays and set up a back office, he would be able to bring in even more business.

But time and the pressures of succeeding at a new business got away from Dad and the long days and even longer weeks piled up. Dad had a simple rule—no work on Sunday. It wasn't so much of a religious thing with him as it was a marriage saver. In fact, he called Sunday "Kate-day" after my mom.

He would say, "If Mama ain't happy, ain't nobody happy."

My mom was always supportive of Dad and the sacrifices he had to make for the business, but she fully owned Sunday as her day. She preferred those Sundays when the whole family would attend church together, the early morning Mass, and then go out to breakfast afterward. As John and I got older, we made it to Mass less and less frequently, but we never skipped breakfast. Rain or shine, we had a seat at The Family Table, a modest diner on Main Street. We were the regulars and everyone at the FT knew us, especially Donna who somehow managed to always land our table. Donna had old-school waitress written all over her, complete with a deep smoker's voice and a tendency to call everyone "Hon." Sounds cliché, but that's how it was. It was all a part of keeping Mama happy.

One slow day at the shop, I was going through "the shop keys" which was a ring of mystery keys that Poor Pete had left behind. I basically tried various keys on various doors or drawers trying to figure out what they opened. I ended up finding a spare key to the closed down wing of the building. That wing featured a small office that looked like a room from a scary movie, so dark and creepy that you knew there had to be someone hiding behind the stacks of old boxes. Then there was a hinged swing door that opened into the auto lift area. I flipped the light switch and it took a good 20 seconds before I heard a low hum and the room was bathed in dim light. There was space for at least four more cars if you cleared all the junk. In the partially buzzed-out fluorescent glow, I caught a glimpse of Dad's vision in that moment. I could see the business doubling if we could get that side opened.

Noises from the other side snapped me back, and for some reason I turned the lights out and ducked down, as if I had been trespassing. That was when I decided I do it. I would clean up this wing as a surprise for Dad and present it to him for his birthday. The trick was to keep it a surprise. For that, I would need help and decided to bring John in on my scheme. We could go over on Sundays after breakfast and make some excuse about plans. Or we could even take turns disappearing during a shift and cover for each other.

And that's what we did. Dad's birthday was in September, so we had four months to get it done. It was hard to get much done during the day, since Dad was there all the time, so we had to rely on Sundays. And I realized quickly I'd have to call in the big guns, so we drew Mom into our conspiracy. As we would wolf down our Sunday breakfast and make to leave the FT, Dad would raise and inquiring eyebrow, and Mom would keep him at bay with a "oh, they've got that youth group thing" or "ah, let 'em go. We need some us time."

It was very slow going at first since John and I didn't know what we were doing and didn't feel super-motivated to work on our Sunday day off. We did some of the surface cleaning and trash removal the first Sunday. I put John to work removing the stacks of old newspapers in the front office and he eventually got bored with it and started throwing wads of newsprint my way. I, of course, had to retaliate and I think we ended up making more of a mess than we'd started with that day. The next few weekends we made a small dent in the clean-up, to the point that I began to be worried about getting it done in time. I insisted John sneak back there as often as possible to put in some extra time since he wasn't directly involved in the actual mechanical repairs, and no one would miss him around the shop. I armed John with a flash light to work by, since turning on the lights in that wing would attract too much attention. I would keep watch and we devised what we thought was a clever signal to notify him if someone was coming. If I saw that Dad or someone was approaching the dormant wing, I was to yell very loudly, "Could you bring me a coffee?" When John heard that, he would know to keep still and turn off his flash light. "That's good coffee!" was my signal back to John that the coast was clear.

Unfortunately, our plan didn't work out so great. John had been in the back room for about 15 minutes when I noticed Charlie push himself out from under a car and head toward the break room, which was right next to our 007 operation. I think I may have overcompensated on the volume when I yelled out, "Could you bring me a coffee?" because everyone else in the shop stopped what they were doing for a moment and looked in my direction. "Please?" I said in a softer tone.

"Get your own damn coffee!" Charlie yelled in kind, followed by a burst of laughter that everyone shared in before settling back to work. I trailed behind Charlie to the kitchen under the guise of getting my own damn coffee.

The problem was, sounds were muffled enough in the back room that John interpreted Charlie's response as an all-clear. His flash light flicked on and illuminated just enough of one corner of a shuttered window to get Charlie's attention.

"You see that, kid?" Charlie whispered and motioned for me to be quiet. "I think we have an intruder." He grabbed a heavy wrench from his back pocket and quietly twisted the door knob to the locked wing, which John had of course left open. "Idiot!" I immediately thought. I should never have trusted my kid brother with this. Seeing as fearless Charlie was about to run in and clobber my brother over the head, I had to come clean.

"Wait," I said to him, pulled him aside, and revealed our plan.

Charlie, when he finished laughing at our half-baked idea, insisted on being in on it. He pointed out a few obvious details that I hadn't considered, like how was I going to get the hydraulics running on the lifts? But he also kicked our vision up a notch by promising that he could not just have the wing cleaned up, but fully operational and stocked with all the necessary parts within the two months left before Dad's birthday. He could come in earlier on Sundays, send Dad home on slow nights, and pull a second shift. In fact, he even wanted to have some sort of ribbon-cutting ceremony to officially open the new wing as part of the surprise for Dad, perhaps invite some key customers, maybe even the mayor, whom he knew personally.

It was a relief to have Charlie in the know and so excited about the project, since he knew what he was doing. At the same time, I was afraid Charlie would blow the surprise, too. He got so into it at times, he could barely contain himself. It reminded me of the time when I was 8 or 9 and I had saved up allowances to buy my mom a snow globe for Christmas. I showed it to John and swore him to secrecy. But the thrill of the secret was too much for him. First, he told mom that he knew what she was getting for Christmas and ran off in a fit of giggles which I then punched out of him. Then, he would drop mom some not so subtle hints by asking her if she liked snow or asking her to find places on the globe we had in our room and saying, "Don't you love this globe?" Mom was clueless or pretended to be so. Finally, on Christmas Day as mom was opening her gift, John yelled out, "It's a snow globe!" and I attacked him, and we were both given the gift of a time out for Christmas.

Without telling me, Charlie let Tony in on our little secret. Tony was a guy my dad had hired fresh out of trade school and we hadn't known him very long. It annoyed me that Charlie recruited him without consulting me, but his enthusiasm won me over in the end, and I began to align more with Charlie's vision of a big reveal.

Charlie did, in fact, invite the mayor to my dad's surprise, as well as a local reporter to chronicle the opening of the new wing. We planned it for the Monday before Dad's birthday. My mom scheduled a fake doctor's appointment for that morning and asked Dad to come with for support. She vaguely mentioned it was something related to her "girl guts" as she put it, and that was all Dad needed to hear. He agreed to go, no questions asked. This gave Charlie and us the time to spit-shine everything and set up a ribbon in front of the door to the new wing for Dad to cut. We had invited some of our regular customers, a few relatives, the mayor, and the reporter, so there was a good sized group of about 15 or 20 people.

Mom called Charlie from inside the doctor's office (yes, even the doctor was in on it) to notify him they were leaving. She insisted on driving Dad to work after her "appointment," saying he could ride back with me that evening. Dad just nodded in his usual "keep Mama happy" way. When they

21

arrived at the shop, Mom insisted on dropping in for a minute to say hi.

They walked into the front of the shop, which was eerily quiet and empty, but a second later the group jumped up from behind the service counter and yelled, "Surprise!" Dad's face went red and lit up with a smile. I think he figured it was a birthday surprise at that point and commented about John being out of school. Mom said, "Don't you worry about that—it's taken care of." As Dad surveyed the crowd, he gave a quizzical look toward the mayor. Mom took charge then and said, "Come right this way, Don. We have another surprise." My aunt handed her an oversized pair of scissors as she passed by and Mom handed them to Dad. "You'll need these." She led him to the ribbon stretched across the door to the dormant wing. That's when my part came in. I had prepared some remarks about how Dad was always giving to others and that we finally wanted to give back. We knew he had been wanting to get the full shop up and running, but didn't have the time. And now, thanks to Charlie, Tony, and some other people, we were proud to present the new and improved Automotive Advantage.

Everyone applauded and Mom motioned to Dad to cut the ribbon. He opened the door and stepped in. "Wow!" was all he could say as he surveyed the room and took it all in. He spoke in sentence fragments after that . . . "fully stocked . . . lifts going? . . . how did? . . wow!"

Someone produced a sheet cake, and the celebration followed. Dad was totally surprised, and we could tell a little proud of us for pulling it off. As much as Charlie made it his project, he was quick to point out that it was 'them boys' idea, and Dad tousled our hair and slapped our backs in appreciation.

I was taken aback when the reporter asked to interview me for his article. I thought for sure he'd be talking with one of the adults, though I was legally an adult myself. He called me the mastermind of the plot and methodically ticked off his questions. At one point while we were talking, I looked over to Dad and saw him talking animatedly with Charlie as they plotted out how to incorporate the new wing into the daily operations. A sense of intense happiness settled over me.

For the most part, I was happy working at the shop. It sure beat flipping burgers at the Golden Spoon. I felt like I was learning a lot and had that mechanic title in sight. When John started part-time in his senior year, it highlighted the differences between us. The shop was only ever a part-time job and a stepping stone for him. He knew exactly what he wanted to do. He'd always wanted to teach and was planning on going to a local university and teaching at the local school after that. So he'd save up all his paychecks toward that goal. I was proud of him for his determination and jealous of him for knowing what he wanted out of life. Sure I was advancing as a mechanic, but

I couldn't help but think there was more out there for me. I just didn't know what.

Photo Finish

Sure enough, we built it and they came. Business took off after the opening of the new wing. I'm not sure why, but this surprised me. My initial idea was just to surprise Dad with something nice, but I didn't really think too far beyond getting the shop fixed before his birthday and keeping my ever-increasing conspirators quiet for the big reveal. Dad absolutely loved having the added capacity and threw himself into making sure we made good use of it. He offered referral specials that might have bankrupted a lesser man, but somehow drew in more and more customers.

I attributed a lot of that early success to the grand opening ceremony. Having a write-up in the local paper really got us a lot of exposure that I doubt we could have come across on our own. And those awesome quotes from me probably helped a lot, too. I braggingly offered this as an explanation years later when we reflected on the boom. In reality, I was pretty impressed with the article about our grand opening. It portrayed me as the "mastermind" behind the event even though everyone else took my idea and improved on it.

The article also incorporated customer and employee points of view, and it informed the community of our presence, but in a subtle way that just felt like you were reading a letter from an old friend. It triggered in me an enduring obsession with the newspaper. I started fetching the paper from the porch even before Dad could get to it and would usually have it read cover to cover before breakfast. John accused me of being an old grandpa, but it did little to curb my habit.

With business expanding and all of us pulling double-shifts, Dad had to bring on more staff. His first hire was Jim, a guy who was mostly self-taught. He had worked at an oil change service as a teen-ager and learned a lot of stuff there. Dad had been impressed with his performance during the job interview, but not so much with his performance on the job. As the weeks and months rolled by, it was obvious that Jim was one of those people who couldn't show up on time if his life depended on it. Dad gave him repeated warnings about his tardiness and sudden and mysterious illnesses, but finally had to let him go.

Then came Eddie, fresh out of high school, so we weren't sure what Dad saw in him. He had taken some night trade school classes while still in school, so we conjectured that Dad saw him as a go-getter. And he was. He went and got himself another job. Eddie only lasted about a month before he handed in his "Dear Don" letter.

Dad really got smarter and more thoughtful about his next hire. First of all, he made the position temp-to-hire and part-time, so we could have a chance to check out the new guy without committing to a big salary right off the bat. He also required a real resume and called references. That's how Mitch came on board.

Mitch wasn't remarkable at first glance: average height, average build, seemed nice enough, kind of quiet, like a neighbor who turns out to be a serial killer. Mitch had worked as a mechanic for five years at a fairly well-known chain in the suburbs of Detroit before circumstances brought him to Chicagoland. He'd heard good buzz around town about Automotive Advantage (or AA as I liked to abbreviate it for effect; as in "excuse me, I've got to leave now or I'll be late for AA"). Mitch initially wanted a full-time position, but Dad explained that the role was part-time with the possibility of full-time for good performance. Dad and Mitch saw the potential in each other apparently, since Dad offered him the role on the spot and Mitch accepted. Mitch got another part-time job or maybe more than one to make ends meet. He kept to himself and we never really knew what the circumstances were that first brought him from Detroit, or where else he worked before he became full-time. John and I made up some elaborate stories, though, including a scenario in which Mitch was a sleeper agent for a super-secret branch of the secret service. The truth was probably much less exciting, and in keeping with my first impression: unremarkable.

Mitch's work ethic was anything but unremarkable, though. The dude never took a break. Contrast this to the rest of the guys whose breaks, if stacked up back-to-back on any given week, would qualify them as part-time employees. Mitch did everything by the book. In fact, he brought with him a series of thick Chilton manuals and actually looked up stuff before starting a repair job that was more involved. The guys gave him a hard time for this. Most of them took a trial and error approach. I remember Charlie letting out a signature gut-wrenching laugh the first time he saw Mitch refer to one of his manuals. "You gotta be kiddin' me, Poindexter!" But again and again, Mitch got the last laugh as he solved the puzzlers we couldn't.

Case in point: Frank's truck. Around the time Mitch started, Frank came in complaining that his 1992 Ford F150 was pulling to the right. Frank was a regular, who had gone to my dad for car care before Dad opened AA. Frank suspected it was a wheel misalignment. We all sort of thought Frank was a car hypochondriac. He was religious about engine tune-ups and suspicious of every noise and squeak his vehicles made. Many times, Dad would send him home with nothing more than a comforting word that he had nothing to worry about.

I was working the front when he came in. Dad was busy with another customer, so I went over to Charlie, who was under a car at that moment. I relayed what Frank had said.

"You drive it?" Charlie mumbled from under the car.

"No, sir," I said.

"Well, get your ass in the truck and see if it's doing what he says."

"Yes, sir," I said.

I told Frank I was going to take it for a spin and asked if he wanted to drive along. He hopped in and sure enough, as I braked at a stop sign, the wheel pulled to the right. Back at the shop, I reported to Charlie, who was still under the car, and asked him what it was.

"What do you think?" he barked sarcastically.

"Wheel alignment," I offered.

I waited for validation, but all I got was, "Well, don't just stand there!"

I headed back to Frank to find him talking with Mitch. This immediately irked me. Frank was my customer. I rushed over and interrupted him.

"Looks like you're gonna need a wheel alignment, Mr. Barrett. That runs about $60 per tire."

Mitch shook his head slightly and kind of cleared his throat before addressing Frank.

"Let me ask you something, Mr. Barrett. Does the steering wheel also shake?"

Frank told him no. I added, "I got this, Mitch. I just drove it with him and it definitely pulls to the right. I checked with Charlie and he said it needs an alignment."

"Uh huh. Uh huh," Mitch nodded. "Mind if I take a look at the tires, Mr. Barrett?" He walked off without waiting for a reply and we both followed him.

This was really starting to piss me off. Mitch was brand new here and I was the owner's kid. It felt like he was trying to encroach on my turf.

"Mitch, is this really necessary?" I tried to whisper to him out of Frank's hearing. He ignored me. Instead, with an authoritative air, he pontificated.

"Ah, I see the problem. Your tire pressure is low on the right. A lot of times that causes the vehicle to list to one side and masquerades as a wheel alignment problem. Jake here will fill those tires and you can be on your way."

Frank breathed a sigh of relief. "Oh, thank you. I was worried it was much more serious."

Mitch walked off and I was left seething, stuck with the grunt work once again and feeling invisible.

Mitch never said, "I told you so" or gloated in an obvious way, but there was always a slight flaring of the nostrils, the raising of an eyebrow, and the beginnings of a smug smirk at the corner of his mouth that drove me crazy every time he proved right in an argument. It got to be so bad that the guys called him "Mitch, the little bitch" behind his back. I must admit, though, that I started that nick name.

All this was lost on my dad. The guys were on their best behavior around Dad. Especially Mitch. He seemed to time his problem solving lectures for the exact moment when my dad was walking by, and my dad always acknowledged him.

"Nice one, Mitch."

"Way to go."

"That's what I'm talking 'bout!"

Granted, these were not over the top compliments, but that wasn't my Dad's style, and I recognized them for the treasures they were. I think I knew deep down that my Dad was proud of me; he showed this every day in his actions. Nevertheless, I envied the kudos he tossed to Mitch because I so seldom got any.

Dad had a way of dragging his feet when it came to closing the shop. On one particularly memorable day, it was a quarter to five and he was having a leisurely chat with Mrs. Willis like he had all the time in the world. Infuriating. Especially since I had not driven separately that day and had told him we needed to leave on time for my date. Too bad Mitch had already clocked out, or he could have closed up.

"You're no good when you're girling, son." Dad had quipped. It was one of his favorite quotes and he used it a lot lately.

I clanked some of the ratchets extra loudly on purpose as I cleaned up in an effort to catch his attention, but Dad was oblivious.

I tried sweeping the shop floor next, getting as close to them as I dared, but they were still rapt in conversation. Ten til. Ugh!

I finally cleared my throat loudly and yelled, "Dad, I'm going to close up the office and turn the lights out," without waiting for a reply. I fumbled for my keys as I entered the office and headed to the register.

Dad had essentially handed over running the office to me, despite my youth. Dad preferred the front office to the back office-it was all about the people and making sure they understood exactly what repairs he had done and how to maintain them and oh, by the way, how was little Jimmy doing in little league and did Suzy like her surprise party? I liked people too, but found I also had a head for details. Dad sometimes forgot to include some of the labor charges or would let the regulars pay on installments that he never tracked. I would point out these little discrepancies until Dad finally said, "You're right, son. Why don't you ring up the next one?" Eventually, I was fully in charge of the register and receipts.

I opened the drawer to find a stack of crisp Benjamins staring up at me with their knowing smirk. "Someone must have paid in cash today while I was at lunch," I thought. "I'm sure Dad doesn't even know what he charged."

I instinctively peeled back and pocketed one of the hundreds, peering over my shoulder as an afterthought. I felt a twinge of conscience, but brushed it away like a cobweb. I'd been doing this for some time and it was easier to justify after awhile. Dad never seemed to notice. His loose interpretation of finance allowed me to do some creative accounting and it just got easier over time.

I pushed the drawer shut, but it didn't catch and swung back open. I gave it another shove. Obviously, something was caught in back of the drawer. I reached my hand in to feel around for the offending item. Something heavier, like card stock, but with a smooth surface touched my fingers-a photograph. What was this doing in here? I shook it back and forth and pulled, tearing the paper a bit as I freed it.

It was a faded Polaroid of me as a kid, perched atop my dad's shoulders, laughing wildly as Dad was reaching up with hands formed into alligator jaws, trying to nibble my belly. It stopped me cold.

This was our father/son ritual, a special bond we shared. No matter how much I begged for a shoulder ride, Dad never seemed to tire. And "gators" were always waiting to pounce, much to my delight. At that instant, I knew I had to confess to Dad.

Tears began to roll down my cheek and a pit the size of a cantaloupe formed in my stomach. I returned the stolen bill to the register and slowly closed the drawer.

"Everything OK, son?" Dad gently asked. I hadn't even heard him enter. I sniffed and wiped my eyes on my sleeve before turning to face him.

"Dad, I need to tell you something."

Dad waited patiently, silently, giving me the space I needed to say what I had to say. That, in itself, was torture and I slumped before continuing.

"I've been stealing money from you."

I braced myself for the angry words I was sure would follow.

Dad sighed heavily and didn't say anything for a moment, adding to the torture.

"I know," he said simply.

Tears formed again in my eyes.

"I could have you arrested right now. I could fire you."

Dad had said these words calmly enough, but it was clear there was a great deal of anger bubbling beneath the surface.

Somehow these consequences hadn't crossed my mind when I was in the moment, but now I realized how horrible it really was. I wasn't a kid taking an extra piece of candy from the porch on Halloween. No, I was a thief stealing from his employer. Whatever would happen I knew I deserved. I would never forget what my father said next.

Dad took a deep breath and let out another heavy sigh, then looked me square in the eyes and said, "I forgive you, Son."

Colorado

My dad wasn't one to linger in an emotional moment for too long or to hold grudges. It never got weird between us and within a few days he was teasing me again as usual.

"Son, you better get ready for that hot date," he winked at me. "You best not keep Rachel waiting."

My mind immediately drifted back to the first time Rachel and I met. I was working at the Golden Spoon, which might as well have been called The Greasy Spoon. It was a standard dive, serving up the usual burgers, fries and shakes. It was the kind of place that had cheesy names for all its menu items: The Midas Touch was the signature burger; Goldfinger was chicken tenders; Goldy-Locks and the Three Bears was a plate of spaghetti and meat balls. You get the picture. It was also well-known to hire a revolving-door work force of high school kids looking to earn an easy buck after school, which is exactly how I came to work there.

I started out as a bus boy, but quickly advanced to kitchen prep work when they saw how expertly I could stack dishes. Actually, I think they were impressed that I hadn't quit after a few months, so they threw me a bone and "promoted" me to a more responsible position. After a while, I would sometimes fill in for the cook in a pinch and before my senior year, I was the official short-order cook for the after school shift.

I first met Rachel at the Golden Spoon. She started as a waitress. There was no formal introduction. One day, I just noticed the new girl through the order window. Waitresses were always coming and going, so I didn't think anything of it (other than that this short brunette was easier on the eyes than most of them).

The first words she ever said to me were, "Where's my Gold Digger, cook?" Kind of romantic, in retrospect. Gold Digger was a double bacon cheese burger with mushroom gravy. It wasn't a particularly busy night, so I was working at a very relaxed pace. It was her first night, though, and she was trying to make a good impression on the patrons. So she felt the need to hover over the counter, which kind of annoyed me, maybe even more so because I should have been moving the orders faster. "Where's my personal space, waitress?" I returned. Her whole face flushed and she walked away. We didn't get off on the best footing, I guess.

Later, she told me she hated my guts at first for

that comment. I would never have been able to tell. She was pretty quiet and reserved, definitely kept her head down and her guard up when she didn't know you. Maybe that was another thing that attracted me to her. She pushed past my rude comment and in time got comfortable enough to dish back the snide remarks I served up. And boy, was she sharp. We started exchanging little barbs back and forth which would become increasingly more flirty.

"You look hot," I would tease, flinging ice chips at her through the window. Rachel just raised her eyebrow, put her hand on her hip, and said, "You look NOT," dismissing me with a 'talk to the hand' gesture.

Eventually, we started taking breaks together and hanging out more. The familiarity between us brought out the courage in me to ask her out, so I did. I did it in a corny, mock-formal way that I knew I could always pass off as a joke if she rejected me.

"M'lady, would you do me the honor of going out with me?"

"I'd be delighted, m'lord."

And so we started dating.

I asked her out on a Thursday for our first date on

Friday. When I got home and proudly announced my date to Mom, she smacked me on the head and said, "Jake, tomorrow's Good Friday, and we're all going to Mass. So unless you're gonna bring this hot date with you . . ." She left that thought unfinished.

"Damn, I mean, darn, I forgot!" I interjected. There was no way I was going to cancel my first official date with Rachel over some church service.

So she ended up going to Mass with us. Mom wouldn't let me out of it, and somehow I convinced Rachel to join us for Mass and we could go out afterwards.

Rachel had been raised Baptist, but her family weren't really practicing Baptists, and she had never been in a Catholic church. It must have been really awkward for her, but she was such a trooper. I had to guide her through when to stand, sit and kneel. And more than once I was tempted to cue her to stand during the kneeling portion of the service, but I knew that would be the end of us, so I refrained.

I picked an Italian restaurant, even though burgers and fries were more my style. I wanted to make a good impression and be on my best behavior, so I kept up the gallantry: opening doors, pulling her chair out, suppressing my belches — that sort of thing. We ordered pasta dishes and I insisted we split a dessert. It wasn't really a romantic gesture, though. Rachel said she didn't want anything and I was about to flip out. Who doesn't order dessert?!

We had started out a bit nervous and formal, but that disappeared with the appetizers, and we never ran out of things to talk about. As I dropped her off at her front door, she turned to me and said in her best hick accent, "Jacob, ya done good."

"Aw, shucks," I said and pretended to blush. "Let's do this again real soon."

We went on a few more dates, and I was really starting to like this girl. I would check the schedule to see what days she would be working and would ask the boss to give me some of the same hours. If I got there ahead of her, I would try to play some sort of stupid trick on her, just to get her attention.

One day, I noticed she was running more than fifteen minutes late, which was very unusual for her. Rachel prided herself on her punctuality. I was beginning to get worried when she arrived with another waitress. I excused myself from the kitchen and made my way over to her.

"Rachel, is everything OK?" She seemed annoyed.

"Yeah. Fine. My stupid car broke down."

"Why didn't you call me? I could have picked you

up. And you know my dad's a mechanic."

"It's fine," she said shortly. "I gotta get to work."

She walked off to change into her uniform and I returned to the kitchen. It was clear she was upset, but didn't want to talk to me about it, which stung a bit. I thought things were going well between us and it pained me to think she didn't want my support.

Later, at break, I caught up with her.

"Hey, Rachel, sorry about your car. I'm glad you're OK. What exactly happened?"

By then, she had cooled off enough to fill me in on the basics. She didn't know what was wrong. The thing just wouldn't start. Her parents weren't home and she knew Judy was working the same shift, so she just called her up. I tried to get her to tell me more about the car and barraged her with questions: What noise did it make? Did it turn over at all? Did you still have battery power?

I could tell she was tiring of my attempt at a remote diagnosis and that each question was just stressing her out more. This was a new side of Rachel I was seeing—a Rachel who didn't know the answer and who wasn't in control of the situation and who was ashamed of that.

I took her hand.

"Look, Rachel. Let me help you. Seriously, my dad's a mechanic and he'll know what's wrong right away. He can probably even do a home visit. Will you let me call him?"

"OK," she said in a small voice. "But I work here, so you know I'm broke. I probably can't afford to repair it, which means I'll probably have to quit. I can't rely on Judy for a ride all the time."

"Hello?" I said, pretending to knock on her head. "It's your boyfriend here. He says you don't have to quit because, #1, his dad will fix your car and, #2, even if he doesn't he'll drive you to work or wherever else you need to go. So stop worrying." I gave her a hug. She seemed to feel better after that.

It was the first time we had held hands and the first time I acknowledged that I was her boyfriend.

Sure enough, my dad insisted on driving out to her place that very night after our shift and after a long day at the shop for him. I drove Rachel to her house where we met my dad. It didn't take him long to figure out the problem, but it would require ordering a part that wouldn't come in for a few days.

I noticed Rachel rolling her eyes as he told her this, not in a sarcastic way but in an "I can't deal with this right now" way. I stepped up.

"OK, so Dad will order the part, and we'll make an appointment to come back later in the week to install it." I said, taking charge.

"Rachel, I'll pick you up for school and take you to work until it's fixed." Anticipating her objections, I added, "I insist. End of discussion."

My dad cocked his head back as if he were appraising me, then turned to Rachel.

"Looks like we've been schooled, Rachel." He laughed and mock-saluted me. "Yes, sir!"

Over the next week, I was true to my word. Like clockwork, I picked up Rachel every day. I couldn't screw this up. I bribed my brother John into making sure I got up early enough since he was the morning person of our duo. Rachel didn't live that far from either my house or the school, but I found myself driving slowly to prolong our time together. Like our first date, we never ran out of things to say, and our mini road trips became the highlight of my week.

The part came in Wednesday, but my dad wasn't able to get over to Rachel's for the installation until Friday. This was fine by me since it gave me a few extra days of car pooling. I didn't want it to end.

On Friday night, as my dad was cleaning up after the repair, Rachel fumbled in her purse.

"Mr. Belcher," she mumbled. "I can only give you twenty dollars now, but I'll pay it off if you can give me a few weeks."

"Nonsense, Rachel," my dad said. "Your money's no good here."

She tried to protest some more, but he wouldn't hear of it. "You're practically family," was his last argument. "See you at breakfast Sunday?"

And so Rachel became a part of our Sunday morning ritual.

I was even more elated when she turned to me after Dad pulled away and said, "Don't think you're getting out of picking me up Monday just because my car is fixed. This isn't over."

From that point, we were pretty much inseparable.

I felt pretty lucky to have such an awesome girlfriend. On the one hand, Rachel was kind of like a brother to me—dishing out the verbal abuse and constantly reminding me how gross I was. On the other hand, she seemed to enjoy my company and was always game for my half-baked date ideas, like the time I took her to the local park for a picnic on the final day of junior soccer league championships. We had to shout to each other over the soccer moms egging on their kids. It wasn't quite the peaceful, romantic gesture I was hoping for. At any rate, our relationship grew stronger and after just a short time knowing her, it was hard to imagine a time when she wasn't in my life.

I guess that's why I was totally thrown off when she announced on one of our Friday dinner dates, "I'm thinking about going to vet school in Colorado."

I knew Rachel was interested in animals. She had two dogs and a cat at home and seemed always on the verge of taking in another stray. In 6th grade, she had volunteered at an animal shelter with her cousin and got hooked. Every once in a while, she would volunteer at our shelter in town and, when it was her turn to pick an activity for a Saturday date, she had me washing dogs all afternoon. That wasn't the part that surprised me. Colorado was. Here's what I knew about Colorado: it was far away and it had mountains.

Suddenly, the reality of our upcoming high school graduation set in. Sure, I knew it was coming and I knew people go to college, often very far away. But I was so enjoying life as it was that I hadn't allowed myself to think too far ahead. And now my girlfriend casually dropped a bomb like this as if it was nothing to pick up and go.

After a few moments of awkward silence, I realized I was expected to say something.

"Really? Colorado? But that's so far away and so…mountainous," I managed.

She laughed at me in her Rachel way and went on, "Yes, Jake. There are mountains in Colorado. There's also one of the top vet schools there."

We talked about it some more and I made it clear I was not a fan of the plan. I couldn't quite articulate why. I mean, she did want to be a vet and Colorado was apparently known for more than just mountains. I think at gut level, I instinctively knew I would be no good at a long distance relationship and wanted to avoid that at all costs.

Over the next few weeks and months, we discussed it a lot, sometimes heatedly. There was one point where Rachel accused me of not being supportive as I tried to talk her out of it, and I accused her of wanting to break up with me. But after our heads cooled a bit, we decided to do some research together. We discovered that admission into vet school was very competitive, so there was no guarantee Rachel would even get in. This gave me a sense of comfort, though I immediately felt guilty for it. Rachel's confidence began to flag, too, as she read more about the requirements. I suggested to her that she might consider studying to be a vet tech, which didn't require as rigorous course work and could be done at a local junior college. I had read that it's easier to get into vet school if an applicant has on-the-job training as a tech, so I talked Rachel into considering going that route. She could enroll in the junior college and maybe get a job at the shelter she sometimes volunteered at.

Eventually, she came to agree with me. I wasn't quite sure if it was my well-formed and logical arguments that changed her mind or if she sensed my desperation at the thought of her leaving. Probably the latter, but I didn't care as long as we would get to be together longer.

As for me, I had no idea what I wanted to do after high school. I knew I wanted to be where Rachel was, but it had never occurred to me to try to follow her to Colorado. What would I do there? I wasn't really interested in four more years of school anywhere, but I didn't have any career path in mind either. Rachel's declaration gave me something to focus on, so I focused on trying to help her.

After we graduated, she was able to get a part time job as a receptionist at the animal shelter. This meant that she worked even fewer hours at the restaurant, so I got to see her less during the week. It kind of felt like I had dodged a bullet with Colorado, only to shoot myself in the foot. But it was far better than the alternative, so I took it.

With Rachel working less and less at the restaurant, my interest also flagged. I cut my hours at the ol' Golden Spoon, too, and signed up for a part-time job at a JC Penney in the mall. That, too, eventually lost its charm and I ended up filling the void with work in my Dad's new auto shop. It was never my intention to follow in my dad's footsteps in the family business, but it kept me close to Rachel, close to my family, and far from having to decide what to do with my life. It was a comfortable path and the one of least resistance, so I followed it.

Here's Johnny

"Mr. Roberts," I singled out the varsity football player who was clearly not paying attention in class. "Please describe to us your impressions of Mary Shelley's *Frankenstein*. You did read the book, I trust?"

"You bet, Mr. B," he nodded. All eyes in the classroom were on him.

"Go on. What was your favorite part?" I encouraged him.

"Well, there were lots of boring parts where the girl drops her handkerchief and faints and writes love letters."

He added dramatic gestures and went into falsetto when he said 'love letters.' The class, of course, ate it up. He continued, "But the part where Frankenstein rips the girl's heart out while she's laying in bed totally rocked. And later, they sew her head to some other chick's body and created Mrs. Frankenstein or something. That was pretty cool." Roberts' disciples laughed together in unison.

"Thank you, Mr. Roberts. That's enough, and it's clear to me you didn't actually read the book written by Mary Shelley in the early 1800s. But you did watch the 1994 adaptation of her book that starred Robert DeNiro as the monster. None of the things you just described happened in the original story."

"Oooh, busted!" someone in back of the room called out to more laughter.

"Crap! Ya got me, Mr. B!" Roberts confessed.

I used that trick every year and invariably some jock fell for it. Roberts reminded me of Jake in a lot of ways. He was popular, athletic, a real smart ass who enjoyed all the social aspects of school, but didn't apply himself too much.

But Roberts was just the sort of student I got into teaching for. I loved the challenge. More often than not, the ones who goofed off to impress their buddies were actually quite teachable if you took the time. I held out hope there would be a pay-off down the road, and they would have a 'lightbulb' moment when it all clicked for them.

For as long as I can remember, I wanted to be a teacher. I have a very clear memory of my first day in kindergarten. In particular, I remember this kid

51

named Tommy who was bawling his eyes out when his mom left. He was inconsolable. The teacher tried to distract him with toys and games and even an extra cookie at treat time. Nothing worked. I remembered my mom had slipped some He-Man stickers into my pocket as I left the house that morning, so I reached in and gave one of them to Tommy. He instantly stopped crying. "What a good teacher's aide you are today, John!" my teacher exclaimed. From that point, I always looked for ways to help out in the classroom. I don't attribute that single incident to my desire to teach, but it served to reinforce that it came naturally to me.

My parents enrolled us in sports from a young age, not because I was interested in them, per se, but because Jake was. Jake was naturally athletic, and I pretty much lurked in his shadow for most of grade school. Jake wanted to do karate, so I wanted to do it too. Our instructor introduced himself as Sensei Kowalski. Any sense of irony was lost on us kids, but Sensei K, as Jake called him, really knew what he was doing. Not just the art of karate, but he knew how to teach. He didn't take a teaching template and force it on each student, but he tailored his style to each individual. He was one of the very few teachers who ever used a different approach when dealing with Jake vs. me. With Jake, it was all hands-on: having him dive in and do, with very little up front instruction. That was what Jake responded to. With me, he was much more deliberate and detailed. He could sense I wanted to know what each belt color meant and the history behind some of the exotic words he would introduce. He would take me aside sometimes to show me the instruction manuals and martial art histories he himself studied from. I was fascinated by Japanese characters, which were so different from English, so he started teaching me some Japanese that he had picked up on the side. In short, I can't remember any of the karate stances or drills we did, but to this day I credit Sensei Kowalski with sparking a love of language in me, further fueling my desire to teach.

As Jake and I grew up, our educational paths diverged. He gravitated toward the sporting and social aspects of school. Coursework was more of an annoying necessity he didn't care too much about. I, however, began to specialize. I took electives: languages, arts, non-required science or math classes, creative writing, and eventually, advanced placement courses. Yet, there was never a sense of rivalry between us. If anything, I think we each felt defensive of each other. If anyone tried to taunt me for being a nerd, Jake was ready with a clobbering if things got out of hand. If I heard disparaging remarks about my jock brother, I stopped them cold with my biting wit. We seemed to recognize and respect our differences with minimal adult supervision.

In my sophomore year of high school, my dad

purchased a washed-up mechanic business and opened up his own shop. I started working there after school in my senior year doing janitorial odds and ends. I wanted to earn some extra money for college, but I didn't want a "real" job that was going to distract me from my studies or, God forbid, my grades. So the family business was perfect. My dad could have gotten by without my help, but he seemed to like having us boys around the shop. Jake had, of course, worked there before me. He even trained as a junior mechanic at one point. I thought he had finally found his calling, but he surprised us all when he took a different path later on. Even though I considered the shop job a stepping stone to the higher education I really wanted to pursue, I still miss those care free days in the shop, working with my dad and brother.

I went to a liberal arts college in Chicago known for its English studies. I could have gone out of state, but I really wanted to end up back in my hometown, teaching in the schools I grew up in. So, I figured it would be best to stay close. My mom was relieved I hadn't gone out of state to a party school, though she really should have known I wasn't the partying type. She didn't like the fact that I commuted to "the city" each day. I think she imagined that I was dodging bullets in between classes or driving through gang warfare zones. Mom just wasn't happy unless she had something to worry about.

She needn't have worried at all. I was the consummate student with little time and interest in extra-curricular activities.

Jake couldn't seem to leave it at that, so he kept needling me about the social life I didn't have. It was as if he was trying to live vicariously through me and experience the college life he chose not to pursue. He would constantly ask me about the girls at school and had I met anyone until finally I had to admit to him that there was someone who had caught my eye. Her name was Allison, a cute, short, blonde girl who seemed to be taking every class I had. What I noticed about her was that she didn't seem to notice me. That intrigued me, since most of the other girls were obviously flirty. From Allison, I got nothing. She was focused, an avid classroom participator who was often at the center of the most lively debates. I tried to interject witty comments into those debates and got a few titters from the other girls, but Allison just barreled right by with her next argument.

I told all this to Jake and he offered me a page from his playbook.

"Dude, you've got to run in to her," he said.

"Well, yes, I see her in almost all my classes," I started, but he broke in.

"No, I mean LITERALLY run into her. Knock her

books out of her hands. I know the type. There's only one way to get through."

I initially dismissed Jake's unorthodox proposal, but the more my witticisms fell on deaf ears, the better his barbaric plan sounded. So against my better judgment, I initiated Operation Jake one fateful afternoon. I waited for a moment when Allison was more distracted than usual—she was reading an early intervention article she just couldn't put down—and I moved in for the spill. I'm not sure Jake would have approved of my technique. It came off more like a badminton volley than a football tackle. But the effect was spot on. Allison looked up at me as if waking up from a dream state, and really noticed me for the first time. After apologizing, I said to her, "Let me make it up to you with coffee." I remember she blushed visibly and quickly gathered up her books and papers to make an escape, but not before turning back to look me in the eye and say, "OK."

Some couples work because of the law of opposites. Allison and I bonded on the basis of parallels. We shared the same interests, tastes, styles, and goals. We immediately fell into a comfortable relationship with none of the tempestuous storms that one so often sees in like-minded pairings. We were the corner puzzle pieces that pop right into place, no questions asked. Allison may have been more intense than me, but a few Sunday brunches sitting between Jake and my dad taught her the wisdom of not taking yourself too seriously (because they certainly didn't). We recognized early on that we were meant to be together for good and talked about our future plans often.

We decided to wait to get married until we both graduated. I would seek a position teaching English in my high school alma mater, just as I had always planned. Allison was all too happy to move to the Chicago suburbs and find work in a grade school. She had grown up downstate in a pretty small town, so the excitement of the city appealed to her. As with most things in life, Allison had a plan for the wedding. My job was to nod my head and say, "Yes, dear." She said it best when I had made an objection early in the planning process that she disagreed with.

"The way I see it," she said in her best homeroom teacher tone, "I've been dreaming about this wedding since I was a little girl. You only started thinking about it last week."

"You win," I said. From that moment it was her show, and I tried not to mess with the details too much. There were a few tense moments with my mom, but in the end everyone was happy. I think we scared off Jake and Rachel though. When it was their turn to get married, they skipped the whole traditional route and opted for a Justice of the Peace wedding. Mom wasn't crazy about that stunt, but it saved Jake and Rachel a lot of headaches and a lot of money.

We rented a Lilliputian apartment a few blocks away from my parents. I had been a student teacher at my high school, so it was fairly easy for me to get a full time teaching position relatively quickly. My graduation, in fact, dovetailed nicely with the retirement of my former English teacher, Mr. Moreau, whose job I had been eyeing since my sophomore year. Allison wasn't as lucky, being an out-of-towner. She went into the regular substitute teaching rotation and picked up some summer school and tutoring gigs, but it was almost a year before a full time role opened up at the grade school.

I have to take a step back and credit Mr. Moreau with instilling an appreciation for the art of the possible in me. I've never forgotten the first day of his English 12 class with what must have been a standard speech for him.

"I'm Mr. Moreau. Spelled like the evil doctor of island fame." He waited for a reaction for a second.

"If you don't get that yet, you will. In case you're in the wrong place, this is an English class. In case you're in the right place, this is an English class." He had this way of looking over the top of his thick-rimmed glasses at the class to see who got it whenever he thought he was being particularly witty.

"It includes, but is not limited to, the study of English. It can be so much more than that, and like life itself, it is what you make of it. The world is your oyster. Someone tell me what that expression means." He took a few comments from the class and wrote the essence on the chalk board. He went on to elaborate.

"The world is your oyster. You can do anything. You can be anything." He grabbed the clipboard with the class roster on it and randomly selected a last name.

"Santos, where are you? You can be a rocket scientist. Too ambitious? How about a bottle rocket scientist? Peterson? You might discover the cure for cancer. Or invent a can-opener. Fenrik? Marine biologist? Surfer dude? Someone else? A teacher? You could teach my class. Someone please step forward and teach my class!" His eyes poked out over the rims.

Sure this was a corny speech and a lot of us surreptitiously rolled our eyes as he delivered it, but in a very basic way the message germinated in my spirit and took root over time. When I became a teacher myself years later, I found myself delivering the same dish to my students—toned down on the idealism and seasoned with the practicality my father handed down to me, but recognizable nonetheless as oyster stew. The world is your oyster.

I guess I lucked out in that my oyster contained many pearls. Not only did I pursue a career and calling that I loved, but I got to share that calling with my wife. We worked and lived close to family and took every opportunity we could to gather together, share a meal, celebrate a milestone, or just chill out. We sometimes talked about what the future held at these gatherings. We'd ask Mom and Dad which nursing home they wanted us to put them in, or we'd place bets on who would give them grandchildren first. I don't think we ever came up with a definitive answer to these burning questions, but enjoyed asking them together.

Blind-Sided

I poured myself a second cup of coffee and sat back down at the table. Aunt Claire continued.

"Did I ever tell you about the time your dad first learned the phrase 'son of a bitch'?"

I smiled and nodded at her to continue.

"He's one who always stuck with things, so of course, he kept saying 'son of a bitch' all the time, trying to get a laugh out of us. It was funny and all at first, but after a while the family really got sick of it. Son of a bitch this and son of a bitch that. It was too much. One day he comes home from school, and Mama wasn't around. 'Where's Mom?' he asks your Uncle Lewis. Now Lewis and he shared a room, so Lewis bore the brunt of his cussing. So Lewis tells him, 'Ma ran off. She got so tired of you saying son of a bitch all the time that she just ran off.' Donnie looks Lewis square in the eye and says, 'Good! Now I can say it all the time!'

Claire let out a wheezy laugh and continued.

"And the best thing was, Mama was standing behind the door the whole time!"

I pictured a young Don, running around like a parrot saying 'son of a bitch, son of a bitch' and nearly spewed my coffee. It was funny to picture my ultra-responsible, conservative dad cussing up a storm, and I realized just how similar we actually were. Sounded like something I would do, too, just to get a laugh.

Just then, Sue Dawson walked into the kitchenette. She cocked her head back when she saw me and rushed in to give me a hug. I stood up.

Sue was our neighbor down the street and was pretty close to my parents. She used to baby sit us when Mom and Dad needed a night off, and we played with her kids in little league. Her son Danny was John's age and one of his best friends.

"Oh, Jake!" She held me there for several seconds longer than I was comfortable with. "How are you holding up?"

I don't remember answering, but I don't think she needed an answer. She transferred the fur coat she had folded over her arm to the back of a chair and we sat down. I introduced Aunt Claire to Sue.

"We heard about it from the Garcias," Sue said. "I didn't see your mom yet, but Danny found John.

So senseless. How's your mom holding up?"

"As well as can be expected. We're all still in shock." I had lost count of how many times I had said this.

Aunt Claire broke in, sensing I wasn't in a very talkative mood. "We were just telling stories about Don as a kid. Do you have any special memories of Don?"

Sue reminisced about the bon fires. Each year in the late summer for as long as I could remember, my parents hosted a neighborhood bon fire in the backyard. Sue remembered it starting out as just an informal get together on lazy summer nights for the immediate neighbors, but soon Don had transformed it into an event by inviting more and more of the block to join in. He would gather all the kids around to show them how to start the fire and would help the youngest ones with their marshmallows. Often by the end of the night, after several rounds of Don's 'cocoa with a kick' for the adults, things got pretty lively. Sue even remembered one night when Don led a conga-line of tipsy neighbors around the fire.

Sue laughed at the end of her account, then sighed. "I can't believe he's gone."

I could relate. I kept thinking with each waking hour that maybe it had all been a dream, and I would drop by the shop in a day or two to see Dad sitting in his office, absently reading the paper. Dad would somehow sense I was near and lift up his head, happy to see his son dropping by for no reason at all. "Get some coffee," he would say. "We got the good donuts today."

I would sit down for a few minutes with Dad, forgetting about the deadlines I had for the paper or the errands I had to run for Rachel, and we'd catch up. He'd tell me a funny story about a customer; I'd tell him the latest joke I'd heard from the editor. He'd ask me about Rachel; I'd ask him about Mom. We'd review the latest Bears exploits or talk about the freak weather, subconsciously trying to prolong the moment of simple togetherness.

John walked up and broke my reverie. "I heard some laughing over here. What'd I miss?"

We caught John up on the conversation. "Remember the time dad set fire to his boot?" he added. I was glad John came by. It felt like I had reinforcements.

"Yeah," I added, "he was telling some campfire story and in his excitement he got a bit too close to the fire. Mom started to say something, but I told her to hush. One by one all the neighbors noticed, but we had some sort of unspoken truce to see how long Dad could go before he noticed."

John took over, "Suddenly the flame leaps up his pants. Mom screams. Everyone rushes over to try to put him out, and Dad just stands there calmly and says, "Whoa! Where'd that come from?"

A few more stories were exchanged before I started to feel guilty for leaving Mom out there alone in the other room. So I excused myself and went back into the main parlor. There I ran into one of Dad's regular customers, Joe.

"What happened, Jake?" he asked me after the usual preliminaries.

The story didn't get easier with each new telling. I suppressed a sigh, and went with my now practiced speech.

"Dad was picking up parts on Saturday afternoon after work. It was around two o'clock. He had just pulled off the expressway for his exit, hit a patch of black ice, and got thrown into oncoming traffic."

Joe shook his head, but didn't say anything. I got the impression he was wanting more than just my Reader's Digest version.

"Oncoming traffic was a semi going 60 miles per hour. He caught Dad at an angle on the driver's side and spun him around before he landed in a ditch. Dad didn't have a chance."

Joe reached over and put his hand on my shoulder, but still said nothing.

"The semi driver was more shook up than banged up and he called 911 right away. I'm told paramedics arrived pretty quickly, but he was DOA by the time they reached the hospital."

"My, oh, my," Joe shook his head again.

"The hospital tried to call my mom, but she wasn't at home. So they called me. I then had the delightful task of breaking the news to Mom and John."

Joe broke in, "I'm so sorry, Jake. Your father was a great guy."

I lost track of what he said after that as my mind drifted back to that day. It had been a lazy Saturday for me, despite having a long "honey do" list from Rachel. Being the ever dutiful husband, I was half-heartedly clearing out some basement junk to make room for baby supplies when the phone rang. I let it ring two more times before I remembered that Rachel was out with Mom, creating some baby registries somewhere. I still had a dust pan in my hand when I answered.

"Is this Jake Belcher?" the voice on the other end asked. I was preparing myself for a quick "No, thank you," assuming it was a telemarketer. Then the lady announced she was from St. Elizabeth Hospital, and my mind instantly flew into dozens of directions, none of them good. She mentioned they had tried to contact my mother, but got no answer. My heart pounded, and I could barely make sense of what she said next; it seemed to come in disjointed fragments of words: there had been an accident . . .Don Belcher rushed to the hospital . . . paramedics tried to revive him . . . head trauma . . . lost too much blood . . . dead . . . dead.

I remember dropping the dust pan, and leaning up against the wall. I managed to hold it together long enough to understand that I needed to get a hold of my Mom, and that we needed to come to the hospital. I hung up and slumped down to the floor.

My God. Mom was with Rachel, doing baby stuff, and ecstatic to be doing it. This would crush her. How can I break this to her? And John. Better to tell John first and have him be with me when I told Mom. In order for that to happen, I had to call John before they got home. No time to think about it or process it. I just dialed him immediately without thinking about what I was going to say.

"Hey, Jake. What's up?" he answered. Words poured out of me because they had to. I barely remember the dialogue, but John told me later I didn't sugar-coat or dance around it at all. He said I used three sentences:

"I just got off the phone with the hospital. Dad was in a major car accident. And he's gone."

He says my voice cracked on the last sentence. After a minute, I was able to fill him in on a few more details, and he went to the same place I had: Mom. I said we needed to both be here when they got home, and he promised that he and Alison would be right over.

We waited in the living room for what seemed like an eternity for them to get home. In the meantime, I had redialed the hospital and was able to talk with the doctor who had seen my dad. I was still stunned and numb, but there was some small comfort in hearing the medical terms for what my dad had suffered, as if maybe naming it and defining it would help me overcome it.

We heard the car pull up and gave them some time to gather some bags. Alison tried to compose herself, but couldn't stop crying, and John just held her as they sat on the sofa. The screen door opened and I pulled the inner door open to greet them.

"I see John is here," Mom said before actually stepping in to the room. As I grabbed some bags from her, Rachel and I exchanged a look, and I could tell in that second that she knew something really bad had happened.

Mom surveyed the room, felt the silent tension, and noticed Alison's red eyes.

"Mom, sit down." I said, and John and I escorted her over to the sofa next to Alison. Her knees seemed to go weak before she reached the cushions.

"It's Dad."

Mom broke down, and then we all did. John and I took turns trying to tell what had happened through the tears.

More people came through after that and brought me back to the present. I dutifully took my place up front by the casket and greeted and repeated. By the end of the day, we were all completely physically and emotionally drained.

John and I tried to keep spirits up the day of the funeral by recalling more funny stories and trying to keep the conversation light. It helped that we had the repast at The Family Table. The owner closed down the restaurant and offered his services for free, which touched us. It seemed like the fitting place for a remembrance meal; we had shared so many good memories with Dad there growing up.

I settled back in, numbly, to my normal routine. It seemed empty, but it was something to do, something to keep my mind occupied, though I constantly thought about Dad anyway.

A few nights later, I had a dream. Dad and I were in a car driving. That was about the extent of the action in the dream. It was unremarkable, but so real. Dad was nursing his ever-present gas station coffee in one hand and steering with the other. He was telling me a story about a trip he had taken as a kid. I don't recall the exact words or even content of the story, but I remember how relaxed it was. The conversation was engaging and mutual and not at all awkward or forced. Laughter flowed freely at times, and pleasant warmth enveloped the car.

I was jarred awake by my alarm clock. The reality of the present screamed even louder at me than the alarm. Dad was gone.

Rachel was already up. I hit the snooze button and turned over. I had read somewhere that some people can return to an interrupted dream, picking up the thread where they left off. I had never thought much about it or tried it before, but I tried it now. I imagined myself back in the car, but already the details were slipping away. There was a fuzziness at the border of my vision that seemed to grow and encroach itself on the vehicle until it looked like a thought bubble from a comic strip. A relentless hammering noise seemed to be coming from the stereo. I looked over to Dad, but the blur had already enveloped him. I listened more closely to the hammering and realized it was the second hand on the clock above our bed. My attempt to return to the dream had failed. I tried a few more times before sitting up abruptly in bed and throwing my pillow across the room.

There was no point in trying to sleep now. I listened for a moment to see if I could hear Rachel downstairs, but heard nothing. It annoyed me that she had left without waking me.

Susan had offered me the entire week off, but I decided I would get back to work sooner. Something to keep my mind occupied, right? I came downstairs ready to get back into the swing of things but was instantly slowed down by the first of many roadblocks: no coffee. Why hadn't Rachel made a pot? She always left a pot warming for me. Rummaging through the pantry, I realized why. We were out. Another strike against Rachel, who had mentioned we were running low a few days ago and had promised to replenish on her way home from work.

The rest of the morning proved equally fruitless. I read the newspaper for a while, which wasn't the same without coffee. I stepped out to the local library to do some research, but instead ended up wading though some dream books. Most of them were new-age, nonsensical interpretations for common themes in dreams. Finally, I pulled out the materials for an article I had been working on about a proposed third suburban airport in a neighboring village, but found I didn't have the energy or will to dig deeper or to make the follow-up calls to set up interviews. What was the point? After milling about for another hour or so, I decided to return home. Even an afternoon nap eluded me.

Several nights later, I dreamed again. I was sitting outdoors on my aunt's patio around a picnic table. My Uncle Lewis sat next to me and Uncle Phillip slid into a seat across from us.

"You try Hank's brisket?" Phillip said to no one in particular.

I did try it then and it tasted better than any brisket I could remember. We talked a bit about Hank's technique and some of the other favorite dishes from the food table behind us. Lewis reminisced about a recent business trip to Kansas City, where he had the best barbecued ribs this side of Dixie. We laughed at his faked Southern accent. Lewis had his hand in all kinds of business deals. Not only did he supply parts to my dad and to many other area auto shops, but he also had his hand in trucking and rail operations and even owned a share in an oil rig. He was the most industrious of my dad's brothers. It was obvious from the glow in his eyes as he regaled us with stories that this was a man who really loved what he did. I admired that. Phillip teased Lewis about being the hick equivalent of Donald Trump, and we had a good laugh over that. I could sense sadness behind Phillip's good natured jabs, as if I could feel his regret that he hadn't made something more of his own life. I seemed to recall Phillip having a lot of health problems that set him back.

From the corner of my eye, I noticed a familiar face talking with some other relatives, but I couldn't place her with a name. She was a short, squat woman with gray hair tied up neatly in a bun. She wore long pants and a shawl around her shoulders, despite the heat of the summer. I kept racking my brain for who she was or where I had seen her, but came up blank. Finally, I nudged Uncle Lewis to ask.

"Why that's your Great Aunt Bonnie," he said. He started telling me some other things about Bonnie, but the dreamscape started to collapse and fade and he never finished his story.

I woke up on my own accord this time. Rachel was still asleep next to me, so I just lay in bed and thought about the dream. Dad wasn't in it, but familiar faces of family and good times were. I thought for a second about trying to return to it, but decided just to stay in the moment. I hadn't really been a rich dreamer up to this point; the dreams I did have faded pretty quickly before I had a chance to recall them. These recent dreams were different. Not only did they leave a clear and lasting image in my head, but they left behind an even clearer emotion. The best way I can describe it is as a feeling of well-being. When I was in them, everything was right with the world. Dad was alive, even if not physically in the dream, and the family was all together and remembering the good times. There was nothing pressing outside of the dream that required my attention, nothing troubling on the horizon. In short, it was safe.

Soon the warmth of the dream began to evaporate, like the covers being pulled off, and I racked my brain the rest of the night trying to figure out what it meant and how I could get back to that place.

Move On Already

I wasn't sure about breakfast. I really liked Jake, but I was starting to feel like things were moving too fast. I barely knew these people. The last name Belcher didn't help. When I tried it out for kicks — Rachel Belcher — it just made me laugh. But I felt obligated now. Don seemed nice enough, and he had fixed my car for free. The only payment he seemed interested in was my coming to their family breakfast. I politely accepted, but I was nervous.

Turns out I didn't need to be. The Belchers were pretty casual and pretty direct — my kind of people. After the first introductions, Mrs. Belcher wasted no time in getting to the point.

"So," she said. "We're all dying to know what you see in Jake."

Jake kicked her under the table and started to scold her. "Mom! What the hell?"

"It's OK, Jake." I said. "I got this." I turned back to Mrs. Belcher and with an air of seriousness I said,

"Who says I see anything in Jake? Not much to see."

John instinctively high-fived me, and Mr. Belcher nearly choked on his coffee. I liked to shock people like that, especially when they expected me to be a shrinking violet type. With the ice broken, our conversation moved on to more mundane topics. I found it very easy to talk with Jake's entire family. Jake was trying to be protective of me the whole time, to shield me from the embarrassment he thought his family would rain down on me. I thought that was kind of cute, even though I didn't need his help.

At one point during breakfast, Mr. Belcher teased Jake about "girling" which was their code for trying to win a girl's heart. I have to admit, I liked the "girling" Jake. He was thoughtful, attentive and a great listener. He was a perfect gentleman, which most high school boys seemed to have given up on a long time ago. He opened doors for me, pulled out the chair, paid the bill. And even though I've never considered myself a girly girl who needs that sort of treatment, I did like the attention.

Jake put a lot of thought into planning our dates. Sometimes it didn't always turn out the way he hoped, but I give him an A for effort. At some point we were talking about our earliest childhood memories, and I happened to mention that mine was of a family picnic, a real old-school affair with a red and white checkered blanket and a basket with sandwiches. I even remembered being terrified by some ants that crawled on the blanket.

For our next date, which Jake told me was a surprise, he drove me to the exact same park where my family picnic had been, and he packed a picnic basket lunch complete with the blanket. He even sprinkled some fake plastic ants on the blanket to recreate my memory. He didn't plan on the park being overrun with a soccer tournament that day, but his efforts were not lost on me.

When Jake wasn't girling, he could be a real pain. Suddenly he wouldn't call or would go quiet when we were together, lost in his own thoughts. He had a way of becoming very fixated on an idea or project, and I and everything else faded into the background. Or sometimes he would talk so much about a pet project that I would be thinking, "Why does he keep talking? Shut up, Jake!" Luckily there weren't too many of these episodes early in our courtship.

Our first big blow up was over my college plans. Somehow, it seemed to take the boy completely by surprise that I would graduate and perhaps want to go away for school. He got it into his head that it was a bad idea. I think he was mostly scared that it would mean the end of our relationship, and I didn't want that either, but in typical Jake style, he dug his heels in on the issue and wouldn't let it go.

I had already decided not to go away, but he was so bull-headed right off the bat that I didn't tell him. I guess I wanted to see how far he would take it. He actually went to the library to research vet tech schools. It got to be almost painful to see him squirm, so I let him think he had talked me into staying local for junior college. It was sweet of him to care.

We continued to date for many years after high school. At some point, it stopped feeling like dating and felt more like living. We were together and we were happy, though we each had our own separate lives. It was no big deal when we moved in together; it just seemed like a logical next step.

I had to smile from the sidelines when John and Allison announced they were getting married. I think everyone expected Jake to pop the question to me first. Of course we talked about it, but didn't see the point in it. We loved each other and knew it and didn't really care what everyone else thought. Not so with Allison. Every detail had to be perfect; every tradition had to be followed. I happened to stop by the Belcher's place on the day when she and Kate were discussing a seating chart for the wedding. Seriously? Who cared if John's coworkers would get along with Allison's second cousin twice removed? I got a migraine just listening to them.

The wedding was nice enough, but the reception

was a blast. We didn't usually have many occasions to dress up and go dancing, so Jake and I ate it up. It wasn't one of those awkward grade school dances where kids stare at the floor. Everyone got on the dance floor. Even Don tried to bust a move.

A few months later, Jake proposed. I was at work at the vet's office, nearing the end of my shift. In walks Jake with Dallas, our Golden Retriever. It wasn't unusual for Jake to drop by with the dog. Naturally, Dallas was thrilled to see his mommy and ran and jumped up to greet me. When I rubbed him under his chin, I felt something different about the collar. There dangling next to the dog tags was a diamond ring.

"Jacob, what did you do?" I scolded him. But he was already down on one knee, flashing me his puppy dog eyes, and asking me if I would make him the happiest dog in the pound. I rolled my eyes, but how could I say no to that?

We had a long-ish engagement, not because there was so much planning, but because I wasn't in a hurry to change the way things were. When we did talk about it, we both agreed that we'd forego the headaches of a traditional wedding ceremony. So our wedding guests were Don, Kate, John, Allison, my parents, and the Justice of the Peace. I let them pick their own seats.

We focused more on the celebration afterwards. I guess that was my key take-away from John and Allison's wedding. So we headed downtown with the family and a small group of close friends for dinner and dancing.

Not a whole lot changed after the wedding, but we were at least official. I think Kate liked that. Jake got more restless with his job. He loved working the family business, but it never quite clicked for him. Jake is not normally a complainer. So when he kept coming home with more and more bad things to say about the shop, I knew something was up. When it got to be nearly every day, I told him, "Don't tell me. Do something about it."

And he did. He got in touch with the editor of the local paper and sweet-talked his way into writing a feature article. I guess it did pretty well, so they had him do a few more special articles before giving him a steady gig as a freelance writer. I was proud of him when he was finally able leave behind the auto shop and work full time as a writer. Plus, he was much more pleasant to be around.

I wasn't in any hurry to have kids. Dallas was all the child I needed, not to mention Jake. My parents, and even Kate and Don, knew better than to nag us about it, too. But about three years into our marriage, I could tell Jake was ready. Not that he constantly talked about it. But I could see by the way he interacted with our friends' kids, he had a love for children and a natural knack for dealing with them. I could tell he'd make a good dad and would never feel quite finished without a son or daughter to call his own. So we decided it was time.

We told the family at my birthday dinner. It was my parents, Jake's parents, John & Allison. We always went out for dinner on my birthday, and I could always count on my mom to bring a cake to the restaurant and embarrass me. Sure enough, after dinner the waiter brought out a store-bought cake with too many candles on it, and I pretended to be surprised. My parents told me to make a wish like I was still a 4 year old girl, and I dutifully blew out the candles. We didn't have the typical birthday wish taboo in my family, so when my dad asked what I had wished for, I simply said, "A healthy baby."

The reactions around the table were the best birthday present ever. My mom teared up and fanned her face. Dad's jaw dropped open. Kate let out a little squeal of delight. Don rose up and clapped Jake on the back. After a round of hugs and high-fives, they all plied me with a million questions. It felt good to have the cat out of the bag and to see them all so excited and making plans. Don ordered a bottle of champagne for the table and an extra dessert for me.

The moms made quite of fuss over me, especially as I began to show. I didn't feel any different, except maybe a little more gassy, so for me, it was business as usual. But the constant attention started getting on my nerves until Jake talked me down from that ledge.

"Give them this, Rachel," he said. "They're excited about being grandmas. This is new territory for them too and they just want to help."

Don totally surprised us at Christmas with a beautiful hand-crafted wooden bassinet he had made himself in the shop after hours. It was stunning, surprisingly detailed and elegant for someone so rough and tumble as Don. The contours of the bassinet mimicked a classic Bentley, and he even included a little winged hood ornament in front with a "B" for "Belcher" engraved on it. And for fun, he dangled a pair of dice rattler from the "hood" of the basinet. We were both floored by it: classic Don all the way with just the right note of playfulness.

About a week later, I was walking in the door with Kate after a fun day of shopping for the baby and I instantly knew something was wrong. I knew it from John and Alison being there. Alison had tears in her eyes, and Jake gave me that look. Someone had died I knew, but I was totally not prepared when Jake told us it was Don. I knew I couldn't break down then. I had to be strong for Kate and the boys. After the initial shock, I made her some tea and saw her off to bed. We insisted she stay with us.

Later that night when I was alone with Jake, he noticed me fidgeting around the room. He came over to me, put his hands on my shoulders, looked me in the eye, and said, "It's OK." That's when I finally lost it. Jake recognized that behind my strong front I was broken up inside. Don was like a second father to me. He was such a strong man. It would be strange not having him around. We didn't see Don all the time. The family breakfasts kind of tapered off after the boys graduated from high school. But there was a comfort in knowing he was a few blocks over. He was the kind of person who didn't have to be physically present to make an impact on you. I let myself sob and just be a mess for a little bit.

There were times that I was alone and let myself really cry. I was really going to miss him. From the first time I met Don, he treated me like family. He was always there to help us out, fix things around the house, repairing my car, whatever we needed. He not only was a good man, but a funny one too. Life was never too big for him. He always had a smile on his face and would put one on yours with a joke or something funny he would do.

I noticed shortly after this that Jake became

withdrawn. That might not seem unusual. He just lost his father after all. But if you knew Jake like I do, you'd realize what a big deal it was. I never saw the guy down or discouraged. He's the most upbeat person I know. I guess I first noticed it in the amount of time he spent sleeping in. Most days he was up before me, even though he works from home. But in the months after Don's death, I couldn't get him out of bed. He kept telling me about these dreams he was having where Don was alive again and they were at family reunions.

I got it. Jake and his dad were close. I could understand his wanting to go back to his happy place. But I was also seven months pregnant and moving a lot slower and needing his help around the house, so it became a real source of frustration. When I first mentioned it to him, I tried to be gentle.

"You gonna sleep all day?" I said, half-joking.

"Deal with it," he mumbled from under the covers. Not in a playful way either. I could feel the tension behind it.

I let that one go, but when he did eventually get up, he was distracted and grumpy and answered only in monosyllables.

"Whatever," I brushed it off, thinking he would snap out of it the next day, but his funk went on for weeks.

One night I hinted in my not-so-subtle way, "I could really go for some chocolate cake."

"Yeah," he muttered not getting the hint or worse, not caring.

I hefted myself off the couch, waddled over to him and pulled the newspaper away from his face. "Jacob. Would you be a dear and run out and bring your pregnant wife some chocolate cake. Pretty please?"

His reaction floored me. He wadded the paper up into a ball and threw it across the room, like a ten year old.

"Dammit, Rachel. I heard you the first time. Fine, yes. Whatever you want." He walked quickly to the closet and grabbed his coat in a huff.

This, of course, angered me and I wasn't going to let him get away with it. "Don't you walk away from me. What the hell is wrong with you?"

"I'm going to get your damn cake. That's what you wanted isn't it?" he barked back.

I told him, "This, whatever it is, isn't about cake. I'm not asking a lot from you, Jake, but I do need you to be here. In the present. Now. We have a baby on the way. A baby who will need his father. And I need you, Jake."

And that's how I should have left it, but I couldn't help myself and added, "I know you miss your father, but it's time to move on."

Big mistake. Jake turned white as a ghost, spun around, slammed the door, and drove off into the night.

Forward & Backward

Mom was hunched over the shop vac, poking at the cobwebs and didn't hear me enter--the perfect opportunity for me to pull one over on her. I crouched down behind the front counter and waited.

Sure enough, Mom's cleaning frenzy brought her next to the front counter. I felt the nozzle zoom past my head, then retract. As it came back around, I lunged, grabbing the hose and shaking it free from Mom's grip.

She screamed, but quickly recovered and wrestled the hose back and began poking my ribs with the nozzle. "You rotten kid!" she laughed. "You trying to send me off to be with your father?" She clutched her heart dramatically. "Quit playing around and give me a hand."

We had been meeting at the shop as often as possible to go through Dad's stuff.

"I'm going to finish up in the office," I told her. "I'm almost done scanning all the paper invoices. Then

I'll help with those boxes. Don't try to move them yourself. Just clean around them."

"Fine," she said, turning the vac back on and shooing my butt out of her way. We worked separately and quietly for the next twenty minutes.

I finished up the invoices and closed down the computer. "OK, Mom." I announced. "Tell me where you want those boxes." She indicated a spot by one of the garage bays that she had set aside for a pick-up the next day.

"I got this, Mom. Sit down awhile and take a load off," I told her, but she wouldn't have it.

"C'mon, son. It'll go faster if we both do it. What are you gonna do for the heaviest boxes, have 'Jake 2' help you?"

"Wow!" I took a step back at her sarcasm. "That's an oldie, but goodie."

Mom stepped up to the other end of the box I was going for and counted down, "1 . . . 2 . . . 3" and together we lifted it.

"Yes, you were quite imaginative as a boy," she continued. "One day, at dinner, you insisted that we set a plate for your imaginary friend. Your father and I played along and when we asked you what your friend's name was, you said simply,

'Jake 2.' Such an imagination and lack of imagination all at once."

"Well, when you've got a good thing going, you stick with it." I offered in defense.

"You and your twin were inseparable. When we tucked you in at night, you wouldn't let us turn the lights out until we said good night to Jake 2 as well."

A sudden pang of grief washed over me as I remembered my childhood tuck-in ritual with Dad. Every night, Dad would scoop me up in his arms and carry me to the bed. On the way, he would pin my arms to my sides and bend his face close to mine to tickle me with his whiskers. I would cry out and squirm, but Dad made sure he got me good. Once released, I would defiantly proclaim, "You're not gonna be able to pick me up when I'm bigger."

Dad would scoop me up again, saying, "If you pick up the calf every day, you'll still be able to pick him up when he's a full grown bull." And he would do curls with me like a weightlifter, making dramatic grunts and going cross-eyed to my delight.

"You alright, Jake?" Mom broke my reverie. "Listen. Let's take a break for a second. I've got to tell you something. Sit down."

"Uh oh," I said. "It's a sit down talk? Should I be scared?" I sat next to her in the waiting area of the shop.

"Jake," she began. "I'm selling the shop to Mitch."

I stood up, "Are you f-ing kidding me? Why the hell would you do that?" My mind raced toward a hundred different scenarios, all of them ending in Mitch, the little Bitch driving the shop into bankruptcy.

"Sit down, Jake." She rose and put her hand on my shoulder and drew me back down. "I knew you wouldn't be happy with it, but can you shut up for a second and listen to your mother?"

I took a deep breath, "By all means, enlighten me."

Mom continued. "You know when your father died, I just wanted to curl up into a ball and die, too, but I couldn't do that. Dad would not have wanted that. So I put on my big girl pants and went into the shop to talk to the guys. They told me how business was going, what they were working on, but mostly stories about the good times they had with your dad. I didn't know what I wanted to do and still don't, but owning a mechanic shop is not at the top of my list."

I couldn't help but interrupt her. "So you're selling out to Mitch? Why not Charlie? He's ten times the mechanic Mitch will ever be, and he's practically family."

"You don't think I thought of that?" she quickly took back the conversation. "I asked you to listen, son. Yes, I pulled Charlie aside and asked if he would like to buy and run the business. But he's old, and your Dad's death has really shaken him, too. He told me he can't do it. And then he told me to consider Mitch."

"Damn him!" I screamed inwardly, but didn't want to upset Mom with another outburst.

"I met with Mitch on Sunday." She continued. "He's a real go-getter. He has a passion for the future of the shop and a plan on how to get it there. He took a few days to decide and accepted my offer. We're working on the paperwork now."

I didn't even know where to begin. "Mom, you don't know Mitch. Sure, he knows the mechanic side of things, but he doesn't have Dad's way with customers. He will run that shop into the ground within the year."

"Well, I don't see his sons stepping up to take over."

That really stung. It was still a sore point with Mom that neither of us wanted to carry on the 'and sons' tradition of the family business, but Dad was always firm about letting us pursue our own paths.

And though I felt guilty still about leaving the shop and knew I could never step up and own it myself, I was still furious at the thought of Mitch once again winning my father's approval, even after his death.

"Sorry, Jakey. I didn't mean to say that, and I don't mean to hurt you. I didn't do this lightly. I prayed to God for wisdom and I asked your father what I should do. I really felt him telling me not to close the shop. Then when I went there and saw how they all worshipped your father and had such respect for him and how he always cared so much for each and every one of them, I knew I had to keep it going. I told your dad what I wanted to do, and I felt him smiling down on me. Later when Mitch and I talked, he insisted on keeping the name Automotive Advantage, and that was confirmation to me that this is the right thing."

I was not happy at all with this. I even briefly considered leaving my writing behind to take on the shop, but I had been down that road once before, and I knew Dad would not want me to do that. It drove me insane that Mom seemed ready to let go of the shop so easily. Somehow, letting go made her feel closer to Dad, while I could feel him slipping away more and more each day.

"I miss him like crazy, Mom," my voice shook a little. "I'm afraid I won't be half the father he was."

"Oh nonsense," Mom smacked my back dismissively. "You'll be a great dad."

"No, seriously, Mom. Dad really had his shit together."

"Language!" she broke in.

"See what I mean? I don't know if I can do it. When my kid looks back on me after I'm gone, what are they going to remember? I was never around? I couldn't provide for them? I failed at my job? My life was a joke?"

Mom gave me a look of disbelief.

"Dad made it look so easy," I continued. "But how did he balance it all? It scares me to think this new life is in my hands and I can so easily screw it up. I've screwed up so many things before that were far less important."

Mom was quick to try to console me.

"Look, son. You won't be alone in this. I'm here. Your brother. Rachel's folks. You're going to have lots of help. And if you think for a minute that your Dad and I always knew what we were doing with you kids, you're kidding yourself. We screwed up plenty. You were just thankfully too little to remember."

I, of course, saw the logic in her words but took little comfort. This was new to me — not having doubts, but verbalizing them. It had been tough enough losing Dad at a time when my first baby was about to arrive. I really did want to be a good father, a good provider, a good husband, but I wasn't sure I had the coordination to juggle it all.

I thought of how Dad would throw me up on his shoulders for a ride and make me laugh in one breath and the next come down on me with some harsh words for getting out of line. Would I be able to do the same — be the fun dad yet still earn respect from my kid?

I always figured I would be an adequate father. But I didn't want adequate. I didn't want average. I wanted to be the best. I wanted . . . Dad. And it hit me that Dad was the missing piece — that I had been looking forward to introducing my baby to Dad, my hero, to someone I knew would keep me on the right track, give me the best advice, be a true friend to my son or daughter. My kid would never know their granddad. And worse, I would never get to present them to him, to say, "Dad, this is my son or this is my daughter. I did OK. Are you proud of me?"

We talked some more and then moved on, under Mom's maneuvering, to more practical topics like feeding schedules and nursery furniture. But I could only participate on the surface as I continued to ponder how in the world I was going to raise a kid without my father's help.

Later that night, I had another dream.

Again, I was at the family reunion. The uncles were starting up a game of horse shoes on the strip of grass next to the garage. I was debating whether or not to join them when I noticed Gail and Clayton sitting in the shade. They almost looked out of place compared to most of the other relatives. They were very put together. It wasn't just their nice clothes, which were not overly fancy, but definitely of some quality. It was the way they carried themselves. Clayton towered at 6 feet something with a head full of salt and pepper hair — more salt than pepper. Gail was shorter with short brown hair. Both beamed a natural attentiveness when they talked with you and a skill at engaging others in interesting conversation.

I approached them with an extended hand. "Gail and Clayton, right?"

"Yes, excellent memory, Jake!" Gail took my hand. "I'm sure you've been introduced to dozens of strangers today."

"I'm surprised you remember us," added Clayton.

I gave my Dad some credit and told them how he had jogged my memory about the "accident."

Gail took up the thread without dropping a stitch. "Wasn't that something?! The 4th of July weekend turned into more of a memorable week or two. Now, let's see, you must have been 10 or 11, and John about 5 years old. You were playing the big brother that day, showing off some newly learned stunts to John."

Clayton broke in with a wink, "I think he was showing off to a larger audience — trying to impress his uncle and aunt, too."

Gail continued, "We were all out there on the porch playing cards and enjoying the beautiful weather while you and John rode your bikes. Suddenly we hear a blood-curdling scream. And that was John, not you. Your baby brother was more scared than you were."

Clayton added, "And with good reason. You looked a mess — blood running down your nose and mouth, cuts and scrapes on your hands and knees. Your Mom was hysterical the minute she saw you."

They recounted how Dad scooped me up into his arms and got me in the house and how they all ran around like chickens with their heads cut off tending to the injuries. After cleaning away the blood, they realized I had busted out my two front teeth.

"When all the commotion had died down, you went to check on John and let him know you were going to be OK," Gail said. "He looked relieved and unclenched his little hand to reveal your teeth. He had gone back to get them because he thought the 'tooth doctor' might need them."

We had a good laugh at that.

"Since it was a holiday weekend and you were miles from home, your mom had a hard time reaching your normal 'tooth doctor.' She was about ready to pack the family up early and head back, but we were able to pull in a favor and have our dentist friend take a look."

"It turned out not to be too serious after all. Your dad had to get back to work the next day, and somehow we convinced your Mom to leave you boys with us for a week longer."

"Of course, you had a lot to do with that, Jake." Clayton interjected. "Once we offered, you begged your parents to stay. We were delighted you actually thought your old uncle and aunt were cool enough."

I admitted to them that I thought of him as the "rich" uncle. I was amazed that he had a whole room in his house just for games and that we got to have soda with our meals—right from the can.

They had a big screen TV, a ping pong table, air hockey, a swimming pool. Why would I ever want to go home?

Gail started up again, "Once your parents left, Clayton and I had a sudden little epiphany that we didn't know the first thing about caring for two growing boys. We never had children ourselves. At every turn it seemed like there was a new issue to deal with."

"Despite the meticulous instruction manual your Mom left," Clayton playfully broke in, "there were so many little unforeseen curve balls we had to figure out. Like when John had a bad nightmare the night your parents left; he was inconsolable. Until Gail discovered what a book worm he was and read to him from *Alice in Wonderland*."

"We finished that book over the next two nights and I had to resort to trying to translate *Pride and Prejudice* to my kid audience." Gail mused.

"We had no clue how to feed you guys," Clayton said. "You, Jake, in particular, were constantly hungry and our practically vegetarian diet wasn't cutting it. We ended up taking multiple trips with you to the grocery store where I'm afraid we let ourselves get manipulated into quite a few unnecessary purchases of a sweet and sticky variety," he winked.

"But eventually we worked through each little challenge together. It was such a fun time. We managed to finagle an extra week out of your Mom in the end, though she never let us watch you again. I wonder why . . ." Gail trailed off ironically and we laughed.

I started to tell them that those few summer weeks were one of my fondest childhood memories, that I never forgot their kindness, that I had wanted to say thank you many times, but then they were slipping away. I felt my body shaking and Rachel was standing over me with an annoyed look on her face. The illusion was broken. I turned away from her and covered my head with the pillow.

Ready or Not

Grandma stirred the pitcher of sweet tea to freshen it up and poured a new glass. "This one's for Jacob," she held it out.

Both I and Grandpa reached for it instinctively before realizing we weren't sure which one she meant. My Grandpa's name was Jacob and I had been named for him.

Grandma clutched her arm dramatically saying, "Someone named Jacob had better claim their tea, before my old arm falls off." She burst out laughing.

I grabbed the glass since I was closer and then passed it over to Grandpa. "Atta boy," he said.

My dad's parents had aged well. Many years of farm living had toughened them up, left them lean and agile, even though they were well into their 80s.

Grandma poured out another glass as Uncle Chester walked up. "Any of that sweet tea left for me, Ma?"

"You eat all your veggies, Chess?" she winked, pretending to withhold it. He made a pouty face and she relented. "Here you go."

Chester sat down next to me. I remembered Dad introducing him as the saint of the family, and my curiosity got the best of me. I had to ask. "So you're the 'saint' of the family, I hear," was my not-so-subtle way of drawing him out.

"Oh I don't know about that," Chester waved it off. "In my younger years, I was a bit of a hell raiser," he said.

Grandma rolled her eyes and Grandpa said sarcastically, "Ya think? As we would have said back in our day, Chester was rode hard and put away wet.'"

Chester continued, "Yeah. You might say the bar was my home away from home."

Grandma elaborated and I could see this wasn't the first time they tag-teamed on telling his story. "Chess drank like a fish. He got into quite a few bar fights and we had to bail him out of jail more than once."

Chester wiped his mustache with the back of his hand, looking sheepish as she continued.

"When he met his first wife, he straightened up for a while, and we thought he'd turn out all right. But then, the drinking started up again and the arguing. Even while Samantha was pregnant with Steven and after he was born, Chester couldn't get his act together. Finally got to the point where Samantha couldn't take it anymore, and she divorced him. She moved out of state, and we only saw Steven maybe once or twice a year after that." Grandma paused for a moment with a faraway look in her eyes.

Chester weighed in, "When Samantha left me and took Steven with her, that was a real wake-up call for me. I knew I had to change. I stopped drinking cold-turkey. I tell you what, that was the hardest thing I ever had to do, and I didn't think I was gonna make it. I knew I needed some help, so I found my way into a church. Turns out they had a group especially for recovering alcoholics like me, and it was just what I needed. I got plugged in. Every time I felt like going out drinking, I tried to volunteer at church instead."

Grandpa chimed in. "That was when the church became his home away from home and he became 'Saint Chester'."

"I was just trying to keep myself out of trouble, and the church gave me an opportunity to do that, and to help others," Chester shrugged.

"And you did," Grandma patted his back. ". . . and through all that volunteering is how you met Deb, and Lord knows that was a match made in heaven. Where would we be without our Deb? And two more grandchildren for us to spoil!"

"And Samantha saw the change in him, too," Grandpa added. "Eventually she learned to trust him again and let Steven visit more often. It's not often you get a second chance in life like that, son."

Chester agreed, "It's never too late to change your stars."

I looked up when he said this, but instead of the sky full of stars that I was expecting, it was the living room ceiling. I must have fallen asleep while watching TV. I looked at the time and realized I had to get a move on to meet up with Beth.

Beth was my half-sister, Dad's child through a previous marriage. She was five years my senior but we were close, and I always dropped the "half" when talking about her. At the funeral, we had promised to get together more frequently, and today we were making good on that promise.

As I drove to her house in a suburb about half an hour away, I reflected on our childhood. We couldn't appreciate it at the time, but now as adults, we had more than once expressed gratitude that Dad and Sue (Beth's mom) had handled the split so amicably and that, at least for Beth, there was no stigma attached to being a child of divorce. Dad stayed involved in Beth's life, and allowed her into his new life with Kate and eventually, us kids. Because we were closer in age, Beth and I bonded quickly. Beth played the older sister with gusto whenever she got to visit—always the Mom when we played house or the boss when we pretended to run our own restaurant. Beth and I conspired together to do experiments on John, since he was the most defenseless of our trio. He was the one we always dressed up or tied up or blamed for the broken lamp. As we got older, John naturally gravitated toward more bookish pursuits and left us 'big kids' to our own devices.

In high school, Beth and I spent less time around each other, but in recent years we seemed to make up for it. Beth had two kids of her own now, age 7 and 5, and I trusted her as one of the few people I could turn to for advice about raising kids.

As usual, Beth was excited to see me, gave me a big hug at the door, and ushered me into her home. She had made sloppy Joes in a crock pot for lunch, a favorite of ours growing up. We chatted casually over lunch, and as we were finishing, she jumped up and said, "Wait here. I've got to show you something."

She returned holding something behind her back.

"Jake, I couldn't help myself. I got something the baby can wear with pride." She made me close my eyes and placed something into my hands. It was a novelty baby onesie that said, "I'm with stupid" in bold letters, with an arrow pointing to the left and right.

"Nice." I said. "We'll have to put the baby in that when she's with her grandparents." I said it instinctively, but realized a second later that she would only ever be with one grandparent, at least on my side.

Beth put a hand on my shoulder. "How you holding up, buddy?"

"Sorry," I said. "I didn't even think about what I was saying. It still seems like one of these days I'll wake up and this whole thing will have been a dream."

Beth was a compassionate ear. She made coffee and we shared some more memories of growing up, separately, with our dad.

At one point, Beth recalled how Dad used to "lay down the law" and how scary he could be when you did something wrong.

"Did I ever tell you about the time I got busted for smoking pot?" I interjected.

"What?" she screamed and punched my arm. "No, you didn't tell me. I knew you were grounded at some point in high school, but you never wanted to talk about it then. Spill!"

So I told her the full story, calling on my journalistic experience to build it up.

"I had a buddy named Dan in high school who was sort of bad news. I'm hanging out with him one night at his house, when he gets on the phone to try to score a dime bag.

When he hung up, he told me we would have to wait a half hour for the pick up, so I followed him back to his room to watch TV.

A few minutes later, the phone rang. Dan ran out to the living room, thinking it was Stevie, his, er, supplier, again. His kid sister, Laura, had gotten to the phone first.

'Mom wants to talk to you,' she said with attitude and quickly left the room as if a bomb might go off any minute. And indeed, it did.

Dan grabbed the phone. 'Yeah?' I could tell right away he was getting chewed out. The conversation went something like, 'What the hell? She's making it up! You're gonna believe her?' It continued, alternating between heated exchanges and long periods of silence during which Dan would frequently roll his eyes. He finally hung up with a 'yeah, yeah, whatever!'

He looked at me. 'Dude, she ratted us out. She must have been listening in and called my mom. And now my mom's calling your mom.'

My heart sunk. I knew Mom was at some church thing, so she wouldn't get her at home. My heart sunk further when I remembered the car phone. Mrs. Ellis had my mom's car phone number and wouldn't hesitate to use it. 'Oh shit!' was all I could respond.

Sure enough, Dan's phone rang again. He gave me a knowing look as he picked up the phone. 'It's for yoooouuuu,' he said sarcastically, as if it were Publisher's Clearinghouse on the line, telling me I won a million bucks.

I don't remember much of what Mom said, but she sure was angry. She demanded that I leave the Ellis's immediately and go straight home. She let me know that she had already told Dad and that he would deal with me when I got home. My heart sunk the furthest yet.

I could barely drive home; I was so scared and sick. As I pulled into the driveway, I knew my time of reckoning was here. I felt that all eyes were on me, that the neighbors had suddenly dropped their rakes and hoses and turned their gaze toward the

Belcher house, and I could swear I heard someone shout, "Dead man walking!"

Dad was sitting in his usual evening spot, a large brown recliner, with his outline virtually faded into the faux suede. You remember Dad's easy chair, right, where he sat and read the paper after a hard day's work, where he used to give us horse rides on his knees and read us stories as kids until we all fell asleep. At that moment it felt to me like the Great Judgment Throne. Dad was seated, tensely, but he rose up immediately as I entered the room and started yelling at me.

Dad had never laid a hand on me or any of us our whole life. Now was no different, though he probably wanted to lay down an old fashioned whooping. The weight of his disappointment in me felt like physical blows, though. It wasn't the words themselves that pained me; I barely remember what he said. But it was his own hurt as he said them that left me feeling like I'd had the crap kicked out of me. And it was powerful enough to get me off pot right then and there. Never touched it again."

"Wow!" Beth looked stunned. "I never knew that, but it sounds like Dad alright."

We cleared the table, and I insisted on doing the dishes for her. While I washed up, Beth fished around in the back room and brought out a few bags of baby clothes she had promised to give to us.

"You must be so psyched for the baby to arrive," she said.

I couldn't bring myself to tell her the truth on how nervous I was, so I just nodded and said, "You bet." She shared some baby stories with me.

After a few minutes the phone rang, and it was Rachel. She explained that John and Alison had to cancel our dinner plans for that evening. She sounded a bit annoyed, but just wanted to call to let me know I didn't have to rush home.

Her call was a good breaking point for my visit with Beth anyway, so I took my leave of her shortly after that. I decided to swing by and pick up dinner for Rachel as a special surprise. I was fully aware how difficult I could be to live with and especially in her condition. Mexican food was just the ticket. We both loved it, and Rachel had mentioned a craving for tamales the other day. Talking with Beth had lifted my spirits, and I felt for a moment that things might just be OK. I had to admit I was excited about the little surprise I had in store for Rachel.

I returned home laden with greasy brown paper sacks smelling of the gooey treasures inside. The first thing Rachel said to me was, "I already made dinner. What are we supposed to do with that?"

"Hello?" I replied. "Mexican!" I shook the bags for emphasis. "I thought you'd be thrilled to have the precious tamales you've been craving. Excuse me for trying to be a thoughtful husband."

"Is that what this was? First time for everything." She rolled her eyes. "Thoughtful would have been calling your wife to let her know you were planning this."

I slammed the bag down on the table, no doubt breaking the chips. This was not lost on Rachel.

"Well, don't throw a tantrum. I'll eat it. I'm just saying we could have coordinated better. You know we're going to have to really tighten on extra spending with this kid on the way."

She walked off into the kitchen to get utensils and plates while I just seethed. I fell to stuffing my face with tacos to prevent myself from arguing further.

Rachel informed me that John and Alison were coming over the next night instead. Rachel and Allison would put the final finishing girly touches on the nursery, while John and I could just hang out and watch the game. I hadn't seen John for a few weeks, so it would be good to have a hormone-free male presence in the house. We finished up dinner in relative silence and Rachel went to go take a bath, while I read up for an article I would have to write on Monday. We watched TV for a bit before getting ready for bed.

Rachel left the room for a moment and returned with the bag of leftover tortilla chips.

"Little late to be eating, isn't it?" I said. Big mistake. Rachel flashed the look. Hand found hip.

"If you want to carry this child, you can. If not, don't you dare say a word about me eating some chips before bed." It might have been my imagination, but I thought she followed it up with a couple of snaps in a Z formation. I thought it best to remain silent, turn my back, and pretend to sleep.

Soon enough, I actually did fall asleep and found myself back at the family reunion. It was almost as if I had returned to the dream I'd had earlier in the day. Grandma, Grandpa and I were sitting around in lawn chairs with our iced teas.

"Oh, Jakey, you'll love this one," Grandma said slapping her knee.

"One night your father . . . How old was he, Jacob?" she addressed my Grandpa.

He furrowed his brows and said, "I don't know. It's your story!"

She continued despite his lack of help, "He had to have been about 16. One night, he snuck out of the house and took the family car out for a joyride with one of his friends. They just drove around hot-rodding, probably girlin' too. A raccoon runs out in front of the car, so Don has to swerve to miss it and ends up driving into a cornfield. That sure cut his plans for the night short. So Don gets home and sneaks back in without anyone hearing him. The next day, Grandpa took the car to the store, and on the way, it started to smoke."

Grandpa took this as his cue to pick up the story line. Their tag team style of storytelling was adorable.

"So I pulled over to check it out, pop the hood, and I notice a bunch of corn husks in the engine. Now I knew I hadn't been in the cornfield with the car. When I got home, just to be sure, I asked Grandma if she had been."

She interrupted him, "Of course I hadn't been! So we gathered all of the kids and asked them one by one if they had used the car. We knew right off the bat it was your dad on account of his squirming the most. He was never a good liar—that's a good trait to have, but it was not good for him now."

Grandpa chimed in, "We kinda tortured the boy by cross-examining the other boys and making him go last on purpose. By the time we got to Don, he started to make up some crazy excuse but realized it was a lost cause and just confessed. Even then he tried to embellish the story, making it seem like he had to go help his friend, but eventually the whole truth came out."

"He was definitely a hand full," Grandma laughed, "but well worth it. He kept us laughing and made sure we were on our toes."

The dream faded at that point and I tried to get back into it, but couldn't. I made a mental note to remember to tell John about this dream. He'd get a kick out of it. I wished for a moment that I could talk to Rachel about these dreams, but I'd tried that before and it went nowhere. In fact, it usually started a fight. She would either take on the air of a psychoanalyst and pretended to lecture me on daddy issues, or worse, she'd accuse me of living in a dream world or hiding behind the dreams so I didn't have to face the baby coming. It pissed me off. I tried to remember that she has a lot going on right now, like growing a human in her body. Even so, she just didn't get it. John would understand.

The next evening was a much needed distraction for both me and Rachel. She and Allison went off to the nursery and she seemed genuinely excited to show off the baby clothes we already had and share plans for the room.

John and I threw back a couple of beers as we watched the game and caught up on everyday life. We soon moved on to Dad things, both still grappling with his absence, both of us trying to make sense of it. I told John about my day with Beth, which triggered more Dad memories from him. We spent the evening laughing a lot about our younger years. I told him about my dreams. I found in him a sympathetic ear with no judgment, which was refreshing.

Before they left, the girls dragged us into the other room to see their handiwork. "Damn!" I said inside my head (maybe it was the beers talking). "It's beginning to look a lot like baby," I hummed internally to the popular Christmas tune. Seeing how they had organized all the supplies and personalized the room really brought this home for me. This baby, MY baby, was coming fast and there was no stopping her and I had better be ready. And I felt so not ready.

Almost There

"I tell my clients that if 80 - 90 percent of what you're eating is in your food plan, it's not going to affect your body that much when you occasionally eat other things," she said.

This was about as far as I was going to get today on the article without additional input from my contact, so I powered down my computer. Besides, it was Friday and I figured I could call it quits a little early. Part of me felt bad that Rachel was still at work, but I quickly got over it. Rachel would be home in an hour or so anyway, and it was her decision to work up until the end. There was no talking her out of it.

Rachel would get 8 weeks off from her job, unpaid. This was another huge concern for me, but thankfully we had savings to work with and were prepared. I say "we," but all the credit goes to Rachel. She started saving (and made me start saving) as soon as we joined our accounts when we got married. This was a steep learning curve for me at first and led to many "honeymoon's over" moments early on. But I thank God she kept us on the straight and narrow. Because of that I could breathe a bit easier on finances.

I kicked back with my feet up on the coffee table and turned on the TV, but very quickly tuned out whatever was on. My mind was racing ahead to a future point a few weeks down the road. I couldn't believe how quickly it was approaching.

I started making a mental check list of our progress. The nursery was done now. Check. We had received a lot of the baby supplies we needed from the shower that my Mom and Alison threw. (Who knew that babies needed special nail clippers or those bulb things that suck up snot?) Check. And the big one — day to day care of the baby. This was huge for us because we both had to work. Since I worked from home, I was particularly worried about juggling child care with my own workload. I'm not known for my razor-sharp focus. But thankfully Rachel's mom stepped up and offered to take the baby after Rachel's maternity leave, so I could work during the day. And, of course, my mom wanted a piece of the action too. So child care? Check. Things were starting to fall into place, but I still had my worries.

When I initially learned Rachel was pregnant, I freaked out. Yes, we wanted a kid (and that's how we always talked about it — not "kids" or "a large family" — always just "one kid"), but now it was real. I was definitely excited, and a little fearful too.   My concerns swung broadly at first and admittedly Jake-centric. Was *I* ready for this? Would *I* make a good dad?   Could *I* make ends meet in this still relatively new career?

Then I got over myself.   Ready or not, here she comes. What would she be like? Would she take the same path I did and be a little hell-raiser?   I certainly pushed all the buttons and tested my parents' patience when I was a kid. Sure, I wanted her to enjoy life, but when I thought back to all the stupid, often dangerous, things I did growing up, I really hoped that didn't run in her genes.

Now that she was only weeks away from arriving, I just wanted Rachel and the baby to be healthy.

Over the last few weeks, I had given a lot of thought to the recurring dreams I was having. In many ways, they were quite nice—reminiscent of happy times and places. There were always stories about the good old days. In one recent dream, I recognized a short, squat, older woman--a real Mrs. Claus type--but I couldn't quite remember how I knew her. Someone told me it was Aunt Bonnie, who was known for baking pies. As soon as they said this, a long forgotten memory came to life. I was about 10 or 11 at one of the reunions when Aunt Bonnie saw me standing by myself and called me over to the dessert table. "You ever had pecan pie?" she asked me. I shook my head. She cut me an adult-sized slice of pie and dolloped it with whipped cream. "Now this is real whipped cream," she winked. "Home made — not that frozen stuff." I dug into the pie and really liked it. I found out later that pecan pie was her specialty, and she had even won ribbons at the state fair.

Like the pie, these dreams were comfort food for my soul, I guess. I didn't want to leave that world and face the real world where many of the familiar faces were gone. Where Dad was gone.

At the same time, I found myself increasingly at a loss over what to make of them. Were they a coping mechanism I had concocted because I missed my dad so much? Some of them seemed to have obvious lessons, like Uncle Chester telling me it was never too late to start over, or Uncle Lewis encouraging me to pursue my passions. Some of them just seemed to be funny stories of my dad as a kid with no real moral at the end. Was there some unifying, cosmic take-away I was supposed to read into them? I would sit pondering what this could be many times until Rachel would wave her hand in front of me and shout, "Hello?! Earth to Jake!"

Were the dreams a sub-conscious how-to manual for raising a family? After all, they all featured family in them. But why was it that upon waking and facing reality I usually felt even less prepared to rise up to the challenge of being a dad myself?

My Dad was actually present in only a few of them, and those were the best. Driving down the road with my Dad, to work, to a reunion, it didn't matter. It was about the journey, not the destination, and I felt safe, comfortable, confident knowing he was next to me. If we hit a bump in the road or broke down, he would know what to do. But even if I just wanted to vent about work or tell a joke, he was a listening ear. Even when he was not physically in the dream, there was a sense of his presence, a feeling that he was just at the periphery of my vision, and if I turned quickly I'd see him tiptoeing up behind me trying to surprise me, or flashing me the thumbs up from a distance and nodding his head.

Just then, a commercial for salad dressing came on, and I realized I better get a move on. I had decided to make Rachel a spaghetti dinner, complete with side salad and garlic bread. It would not be enough to make up for the way I'd treated her lately, for my angry outbursts and for being checked out, but it was a start. The dreams, and whatever I was supposed to get from them, would have to wait.

The Keys

I was telling Grandma and Grandpa another story when I felt a hand on my shoulder. It was Dad and he said, "It's OK. Go on with the story. I'm just letting you know it's time to get going in a bit." I wound it up and Dad announced, "Well, we should be heading back now. Long drive ahead of us."

I had totally lost track of the time, but sure enough the sun was sinking in the sky and casting long shadows on the cornfields. We initiated the "long goodbye" with hugs all around, squeezing in one last story or joke, promising to keep in touch more frequently throughout the year, knowing that we probably wouldn't and that that was ok, too.

Aunt Bonnie fussed over making us plates of leftovers to go and we graciously accepted her overstuffed plates and Tupperware, even though we were already stuffed ourselves. We made our rounds of goodbyes slowly in the fading light, none of us really wanting the day to end. Dad finally had to call a truce and dragged me away from Grandma's bear hug. We waved, walking backwards until the side of the house blocked our view of the family.

I headed to the passenger side of the car and was waiting for Dad to unlock it. But he didn't. I looked up to see him smiling at me strangely over the roof of the car. Without warning, he flipped me the keys. I had to shift my plate of leftovers to my other hand, but made the catch, barely.

"Atta boy," he said. "Why don't you drive us home?"

We switched places and I got in the driver's seat.

We drove in silence for a few minutes, letting the rhythm of the road cradle our thoughts.

"How is she doing?" Dad broke the silence. Somehow, I knew he was talking about Rachel and our baby girl all at once. And behind the question, he was really asking about me.

"I don't know," I started and suddenly the floodgates opened and all my doubts and worries of the past nine months came pouring out. Holy crap, I was going to be a father. And I didn't feel ready. Worries about money and insurance and child care logistics swirled in with fears about how everything would change, how our relationship would change, how I would be responsible for this tiny new life with my own so screwed up. I tried to make sense of my dreams. I tried to analyze the choices I'd made in life, to dissect my childhood, to forecast my future. I don't remember exactly what I said, but it ended with a choking sound in my throat as I said, "And I don't know how I can do it without you, Dad."

I suddenly felt ashamed of my outburst and looked straight ahead at the winding pattern of lights on the road. It seemed like the street would be swallowed up in darkness, but without fail a light would appear further off on the horizon and would steadily grow brighter until the next one showed itself.

"Son," my Dad replied. "You know I'm always here."

I looked over and he was gone.

The street lamps were gone. The bags of leftovers were gone, replaced by an overnight bag on the passenger seat with some extra items for Rachel. She had delivered our beautiful baby girl the day before at 11:07 am, 7 pounds, 10 ounces, 21 inches long. My God, she was beautiful! I was heading back to the hospital now to see her again. She had a full head of black hair, dimples in both cheeks, and a knowing twinkle in her eyes. Grandpa's eyes.

I knew we would be just fine.

The journey continues... *RandyBeal*.com

www.ingramcontent.com/pod-product-compliance
Lightning Source LLC
Chambersburg PA
CBHW060437130626
46555CB00005B/2402